Captain Bloody Bill Walker
and
The Letter of Marque

Doc Hanson

Copyright © 2015 Doc Hanson
All rights reserved
First Edition

PAGE PUBLISHING, INC.
New York, NY

First originally published by Page Publishing, Inc. 2015

ISBN 978-1-68139-183-0 (pbk)
ISBN 978-1-68139-184-7 (digital)

Printed in the United States of America

Contents

A Ship at Peace 7
The Magdalena 11
Pieces of Eight 14
Prize Crew 22
Boucanier's Celebration 26
The Spanish Admiral 33
A Contrabano Ship 42
Catlina 51
Raid on La Habana 61
Come to Quarters 72
Lloyd's Coffeehouse 75
Sir Harold Dobbs 77
A Purse Filled with Gold 91
Captain Mansvelt 94
Recruiting a Crew 100
A Dandy Young Wench 109
Governor Modyford Arrives 113
Captains of the Coast 118
The Island 126
A Privateer Port 130
Secret Code 143
Lilly 147
Raid on Providence 151
Río de la Muerte 157
Smoke and Oakum 164
Postscript 171

From: Sir Thomas Modyford, Baronet, Governor in and over His Majesty's Plantations & Properties of the Island of Jamaica, and Commander in Chief of all His Majesty's Forces within said Island and Islands adjacent, vice-Admiral to His Royal Highness the Duke of York's Ships and Navies in The Americas, &c &c

Be It Known To All and to Captain William Walker, R.N. Greetings,

Whereas, by His Majesty's Commission under the Great Seal of Great Britain bearing Date the 13th Day of April in the year of Our Lord 1660, and in the 11th Year of His Majesty's Reign, the Office of Lord High Admiral, the Duke of York are required and authorized to issue forth and grant Letters of Marque and Reprisal to any of His Majesty's Subjects or others, whom we shall deem fitly qualified in that Behalf for apprehending, seizing, and taking the Ships, Vessels and Goods belonging to any person, nation or country with hostile intent or actions against any of His Majesty's Subjects, properties, or possessions, or to any Persons being Subjects of the Parties (save and except for any Ships to which license has been granted) and to bring the same to Judgment in any of His Majesty's Courts of Admiralty with his Dominions, for Proceedings and Adjudication and Condemnation to be thereupon had, according to the Court of Admiralty, and the Laws of Nations; These are, therefore, to will and require me to cause an Order of Marque and Reprisals to be issued out of the High Court of Admiralty unto Captain William Walker, Master and Commander of the Dutch Costal Trade, Commencement. Burthern of about one hundred tons, mounted with ten Carriage Guns carrying Shot of twelve & nine Pounds Weight inaddition of Four Swivel Guns and navigated with Seventy men, whereas the said Captain Walker is commander, to apprehend, seize, and take any Ships, Vessels, Lands or Ports and Goods Belonging to hostile nations, or to any persons being Subjects of these hostile nations, according to His Majesty's Commission and Instruction aforesaid. And to keep an exact Journal of Proceedings, and therein particularly to take notice of all Prizes taken, the nature of such Prizes, the Time and Place of their being taken, the value of them as near as can be judged, as also the Situation, Motion and Strength of the Spanish, as well as can be discovered by the best Intelligence available; of which shall from Time to Time, as shall the Opportunity present, to transmit an Account to our Secretary. Provide always that security be given according to His Majesty's Instructions before mentioned; the Said Letters of Marque and Reprisal to continue in force until further orders, for which this shall be Warrant.

Given under my Hand, and the Great Seal of the Island of Jamaica this 19th day of November 1666 and in the name of His Majesty and,

By My Command.

Thos. Modyford

A Ship at Peace

18 July 1663, 5:00 p.m.
the Caribbean
21° north latitude

The small squadron of ships would have been a credit to any navy had they not been sea rovers. The *Commencement* had originally been a Dutch two-masted coastal trader built in the Netherlands in 1651. She was clinker-built with strakes that overlapped her hull instead of the more popular, cheaper carvel-built ships, where boards just abutted against each other. Her heavy oak hull was double-planked. She was one hundred tons burthen with a length of eighty feet and a twenty-two-foot beam. Her draught of only eight feet seven inches allowed her to skim wistfully across the shallow blue waters of the West Indies. She was brigantine with both square rigging and fore and aft sails that hung from her two tall masts. The new ship's master carpenter, Alonso Sanchez, had made flush the decks by removing the forecastle and lowering the quarterdeck. A flush deck without a break or step in the weather deck provided an unobstructed fighting platform. He had also removed the bulkheads or interior walls below deck to clear space for working the additional heavy carriage guns that had been brought aboard after her capture. The *Commencement* was now a predator. The Caribbean was her new home. She was a British privateer commanded by Captain William Walker.

A French twenty-eight under the command of Lieutenant Andre Brossard was anchored two cable lengths off the *Commencement's* starboard bow. Her crew had mutinied off the coast of Madagascar and then sailed under the tip of Africa and crossed the Atlantic to the Caribbean. The square-masted frigate was now being transformed by Alonso, the Basque carpenter, and fifteen other skilled craftsmen for her new role as a sea rover. The sixth-rate ship of the line would be renamed the *Blanche Sorciere*—the *White Witch*.

A single-masted barque was careened on the nearby white, sandy beach, her hull exposed to the hot tropical sun. Men were at work scraping her hull to remove the barnacles and seaweed that had accumulated over the months of sailing in the warm, rich waters of the Caribbean. The *Nancy* was slim and light in comparison to the other two vessels in the squadron with only four bronze swivel guns mounted on the gunwales. But she played her part in the fleet by being able to sail close to the wind for speed, maneuvering without fault on the open sea and then drifting silently along the coastal shoals and into inlets and rivers from where she could attack lazy merchant ships carrying rich cargos without a watch.

Privateers—unlike the Royal Navy, the East India Company, Royal Africa Company, or New Bedford whalers—could not have ships built to order. They were captured prize vessels that were then cut down and refitted. They were not large cargo vessels designed for long voyages or heavily armed warships. They were sturdy, low freeboard, swift, rakish, predatory vessels that could attack without warning and then escape up rivers or hide among the tidal shoals and inlets. The usually silent, uninhabited island's lagoon where the ships rested was alive with activity and the sounds of men working.

The *Commencement* lay at single anchor in motionless beauty. Her sides were painted black. One small narrow ribbon of red was painted just above the sweep ports. The galley-like sweep ports or oar ports could be opened to allow the use of long oars in calms and rivers or to row silently alongside an anchored ship in the still of the night. Her decks were Jamaican red cedar. Overhead hung white awnings fore and aft to protect the crew from the sun while she lay at anchor. Her hemp lines and cables were hauled taut against white mask, and her dark blue damask sails were tied against white spars.

On the starboard and larboard sides of the dark red-cedar deck, four brightly polished, five-foot-long, nine-pound, bronze Cromwell cannons rested in heavy mahogany carriages. With the foredeck removed, a similar nine-pounder chase gun was placed at the bow.

Belowdecks, four nine-pounders peeped out of open gunports. Ominous looking thirty-three-inch, copper banded, Chinese dragon swivel guns were mounted two astern and two forward. The oiled iron barrels were etched with silver figures of seahorses, fish and Chinese symbols. Each of these deadly weapons could fire three-fourths of a pound of grapeshot.

Captain Walker stood on the elevated quarterdeck looking over the taffrailing down into the calm, crystal clear sea. Through the clear water, her copper and brass shone brightly, and he could plainly discover the white, sandy bottom beneath and the anchor that lay under her counter. As the sun set, faint shadows from the mast, binnacle, and ship's wheel spread across the deck. The red English ensign hung loosely at her stern. The flag catching the gentle breeze at the crest of her main mast was black.

Walker heard the ship's bell ring twice. While the crisp notes of the bell echoed across the placid island's cove, Mr. Burke, the boatswain, piped, "Call to supper!" A crew of seventy able-bodied seamen came on deck. The large crew of the *Commencement* and the other ships in the squadron had come together for the privateering season, which, in the Caribbean, lasted a few months starting in April. These few months were ideal because the winds were fair, the seas were calm, and the weather was good. And most importantly, it was during these months that the Spanish convoys carried treasure back to Spain. Privateering was not a full-time job. It was seasonal. During most of the year, many of the men lived onshore either running small businesses or signing on *contrabano* ships that ran the blockades to carry smuggled goods from one island to another, selling their cargo to the highest bidder.

No single nationality stood out onboard the *Commencement*. The crew was a mix of English, Irish, Scottish, French, Negro, Creole, and Miskito Indians. There were no indentured landsmen or slaves aboard. They were all considered *boucaniers*. They were all experienced seamen, and they were all sea dogs sailing under letters of reprisal issued by the governor of Jamaica. The crew had signed on for shares in any prize captured or taken during the voyage, on land or at sea.

As Captain Walker ambled down the steps from the quarterdeck to his cabin, he was thinking about the information he had received concerning the Spanish convoy from the Gypsy girl, Catlina, and what might lie ahead for the ships in his small squadron as they made plans to attack that convoy.

"Marcum, Marcum!" Bill called, knowing that his steward was probably lurking around someplace close. "Marcum!"

"Aye, sir," the steward answered as he came into the cabin.

"Would you relay my compliments to Lieutenant Brossard and kindly ask him to join me, if he is available," Bill said to Marcum.

"Aye, sir," he responded briskly, and then turning, he walked away, grumbling to himself in a low voice, "Compliments to Mr. Brossard and ask if he can join you."

The Magdalena

*18 July 1663, 8:00 p.m.
the Caribbean
16° north latitude*

The *Magdalena* flew a good deal faster now, the Spanish admiral noticed. He had adjusted the trim and reshifted the ballast. Sitting on the open-air gallery just outside his cabin, Juan Martinez de Palategui saw that the sea had barely a ruffle on its surface. But looking up, he noticed that the ship's topgallants grabbed enough wind to push the vessel in a long, straight furrow across the water. Her wake drew a dim white-blue line of phosphorescence that was visible for several leagues behind the ship. Juan Martinez, unlike other Spanish captains or admirals at the time, was more of the intellectual and scholar than a warrior. But he understood sailing ships, and at the end of the sixteenth century, a new type of warship emerged from Spain—the galleon. He had studied and knew this ship well. His galleon weighed one thousand *toneladas* burden with four tall masts. It was stronger, bigger, and more heavily armed than any other ship had ever been, and the admiral knew that his fleet of galleons had but one purpose. They were battleships.

The galleon had a different hull from the older carrack. The new hull had a greater length-to-keel and length-to-beam ratio (4:3:1 as opposed to the carrack's 3:2:1), which made the hull's reach long and narrow, thus improving the flow of water around its base, reducing resistance at the waterline, and giving the ship better maneuverability. Also, the old carrack's round stern was chiseled into a narrower flat end that supported the weight of the aftcastle better. Galleries, open-air balconies went around the whole stern portion of the ship and extended on the sides to the mainmast chains, where the shrouds were attached to the hull.

The excessive bulk of the forecastle and aftcastles on the carrack had hindered their sailing characteristics, so the forecastle on the galleon was moved from above the stem to a position behind it, with the bowsprit poking out from its bow, reducing the chance of wind hitting the forecastle and turning the ship unintentionally. With the forecastle pushed farther back, the stem extended farther out underneath the bowsprit, forming an elaborate tapering outline that was decorated with a figurehead. And in the dead space of this new addition, the head was formed. These changes enabled a galleon to sail considerably closer to the wind and thus increased her speed. The admiral's fleet of galleons could easily make twelve knots. Twelve knots was an incredible speed for a ship this size.

The need of ever-heavier cannons on several decks as well as the need to otherwise increase the cargo capacity of the ships led to the use of hull frames, braces, and knees under the decks that made the hull wide at the waterline but then tapered inward in order to take the weight of the guns belowdecks as close to the centerline as possible and thus improve the stability. A single galleon could carry forty guns or more. The *Magdalena* carried eighteen culverins on the lower deck, fourteen demiculverins on the upper deck, and eight sakers. The tapering hull also had the added advantage of making boarding the ship more difficult from an adjacent enemy ship.

The *Magdalena's* four heavy masts were made from oak and wrapped tightly with bands of copper for added strength. The large billowing sails, common on older vessels, had been recut into flatter square sheets that further improved her sailing capabilities. Topmasts could be added to the foremast and the mainmast. If the winds were right a large floating second mizzen, aft of the first, called a bonaventure, could also be rigged.

The Spanish galleon was the undisputed master of all the waters from the Bay of Honduras to the Windward Islands. This part of the Caribbean was known as The Spanish Main. But galleons like the *Magdalena* also commanded the waters from Cape Sable in Florida along the coastline to Trinidad. It was once called the Spanish Lake but was later renamed the Gulf of Mexico. Past the Windward Islands south along the coastline of South America were Portuguese waters. By treaty the Portuguese held most of South America and the Spanish galleon was seldom seen in these waters. The Portuguese also commanded the sea trade lanes across the Indian Ocean to China and the Spice Islands. But the Spanish galleon ruled the South Seas and carried the fabulous cargos of the orient from their seaport in Manila across the Pacific to land at Panama. Most of the silver coins minted in the New World found their way into three-lock sea chests that were placed aboard a Manila Galleon. From Panama the fleet of galleons sailed back across the South Sea to Philippians where the silver was used to purchase the rich merchandise that was only available in these lands.

"Entrada!" Martin shouted to the soldier standing outside his cabin door.

The guard entered. "Your Excellency, Captain Barcenas to see you," the orderly announced.

"Show the captain in."

Barcenas cautiously entered the large ornate cabin on the upper deck just under the high aftcastle, the admiral asked but one question. "I believe that these pirates will attack our convoy tomorrow. Is the decoy ship positioned as I have ordered?"

"Yes, Your Excellency."

"And does her captain know what he is to do when they attack?"

"Yes, Your Excellency. I have given him your instructions."

Pieces of Eight

18 July 1663, 9:00 p.m.
the Caribbean
21° north latitude

Lieutenant Brossard found Captain Walker in his cramped low-ceiling quarters aboard the *Commencement,* standing over a small table, studying a few crude hand-drawn nautical charts. "Lieutenant Brossard, you are well, I trust?" asked Bill as Brossard entered his quarters.

"My compliments, Captain. May I inform you that the lookout on the island has spied Spanish ships, but none the taking, I'm afraid. I have also received notice from one of our scout ships that the treasure fleet is one day's sail from us."

"Has Alonso completed the work on your ship?" asked Bill.

"Aye, sir. The work on the *Sorciere* will be completed by tomorrow morning. Her guns are back onboard. She can be fitted out and ready to sail tomorrow," Brossard said as he walked casually around the table, looking at the maps. "That Basque carpenter knows what he's doing. She looks like a different ship. No one will ever recognize her as a French naval vessel."

Brossard had been a French naval officer on the verge of dismissal from service for larceny and a few other offences before he set against the captain and officers of his own vessel. Taking command of the ship, he killed all but a few willing hands necessary to man the vessel and sailed for the West Indies; discarded and without means but with a captured ship, he came to the attention of Captain Walker.

Master Shipbuilder Alonso Sanchez began tearing the vessel apart and rebuilding her as a privateer as soon as the French ship came under Bill's command. A mutineer, Brossard was no better or worse than any other scoundrel that fled to the West Indies.

"A day's sail away, you say?" commented Bill.

"Marcum, Marcum!" Bill called again.

"Aye, sir?" Marcum mumbled.

"Would you relay my compliments to Mr. Cribb and kindly ask him to join us also, if he is available."

"Aye, sir," Marcum responded meekly and shuffled out of the cabin.

After being in these waters since the year '55, Bill knew that the Caribbean was in many ways a paradise for a privateer. The string of large and small islands stretching in an arc from the Florida Keys to Trinidad and Tobago enjoyed a sunny climate, which was in stark contrast to the gray skies and cold winters of the North Atlantic that he had sailed in as a midshipman in the King's Navy. Or the energy-draining heat and humidity he had endured as a master's mate along the coast of Africa. The mild warm sun of the Caribbean was tempered by gentle breezes and plentiful rain, ensuring an abundant growth of tropical plants, trees, and shrubs on land. His ships dropping anchor in any one of the thousands of bays and lagoons usually had little difficulty finding freshwater and food. There were sheltered coves in the hundreds of deserted islands where a ship could hide for weeks undetected and shelving white-sand beaches where vessels like his sloop could be run ashore so that she could be repaired and cleaned of seaweeds and barnacles. A clean ship ran faster through the water. Speed and, of course, surprise were what gave the privateer ships the advantage against the heavily armed Spanish and Dutch warships.

But the Caribbean, as appealing as it might seem at first, had many serious disadvantages. Hurricanes and tropical storms that seemed to come out of nowhere wreaked havoc both on land and at sea and could destroy everything in their path. Mosquitoes and sandflies were rife, particularly among the mangrove swamps, which were often found on many of the islands. And most deadly of all were the diseases. Malaria, yellow fever, and other calentures (fevers) were the chief killers, but there were also deaths from catarrhs like influenza. Also consumption, pneumonia, dysentery, dropsy, and some diseases brought over from Africa, such as guinea worm and leprosy. But by and large, the crew was well fed and healthy, and the Caribbean was an ideal place for a privateer carrying the red British ensign. And best of all was that when his small squadron captured a Spanish or Dutch ship or raided a settlement, it was legal. What would have been considered an act of piracy was legal under English law because Captain Walker was acting on behalf of the Crown and the Admiralty as a private man-of-war under a letter of marque and reprisal.

William Walker was the eldest son of William Senior and Frances Walker from Poole, a small but prosperous seaport in Dorset, on the southern coast of England. His father was master of his own ship and had shares in a number of other ventures and was a successful captain in the shipping trade on which the prosperity of Poole was based. Situated at the head of the largest natural harbor in England, the port had established a flourishing trade with the Newfoundland cod fisheries in North America. Ships sailed from Poole to Newfoundland with cargoes of salt and provisions; they exchanged these for dried and salted fish and sailed back across the Atlantic to European ports where they sold the fish and returned to Poole with cargoes of wine, brandy, olive oil, and leather pouches filled with Spanish silver reales and gold escudos. Bill's mother died when he was five years old, and he was raised onboard ships, accompanying his father on these voyages across the Atlantic as well as sailing with his father down the coast of Africa. Though Bill would never discuss the nature of his father's trips to Africa, it was well understood that they probably involved the slave trade.

On this day in July, Walker's ships were anchored off an island that lay at almost exactly 21° north latitude and inside the Windward Passage between Cuba to the northwest and Hispaniola to the northeast. Twice a year, fleets of fifty to one hundred treasure-laden Spanish ships guarded by heavily armed galleons sailed through the Windward Passage to make their last stop at Havana for refitting and victualling before crossing the Atlantic to Seville in Spain. Because of favorable winds and currents, the returning flotilla from the Spanish Main had to sail through this Windward Passage. The retuning flotillas from places farther north like Vera Cruse sailed the Northward Passage, hugging the southern coast of the Gulf of

Americas to Cuba. But on this day, the *Commencement,* her crew, and the other ships waited in a sheltered cove off the Windward Passage.

The Spanish trade with the West Indies flourished, and taxes for Spanish colonies in the New World increased every year. There were now a hundred thousand Spaniards and their descendents living in New Spain and three hundred thousand living in South America. But the riches of the New World were unbelievable. At Potosi in Bolivia, there was tell of a mountain fifteen thousand feet high made of silver. The Aztec and Inca treasures discovered by Cortes and Pizarro were so large that the Spanish established a mint for converting the precious metals into coins. Solid silver eight-peso coins called pieces of eight by the English and gold doubloons were shipped back to Spain by the tons. All silver coins were actually called reales, and a peso was eight reales. Gold coins were called escudos. The 6.7-gram double escudo or eight escudos was called a doubloon, which was the highest value Spanish coin now in circulation. Each silver peso was worth four shillings and sixpence in England. There were so many minted coins coming back to Europe from the New World that the peso and escudo became the currency standard of the world. One Spanish galleon might carry one hundred cases of gold ingots and minted gold escudos, each case weighing five hundred pounds; tons of silver ingots and pieces of eight; five hundred pounds of gold dust in bags; pearls, emeralds, rubies, and topaz gems in barrels weighing 680 pounds each; Aztec and Inca native jeweled gold and silver rings, necklaces, bracelets; golden mask and helmets set with gems and feathered cloaks. And then there was the French 23-carat gold pieces weighing almost one ounce each called Louie's or Louis d'or's and large heavy Dutch silver guilders that could also be captured. The shares of one captured Spanish treasure galleon, prize vessel, could set the captain and crew ashore in comfort and style for life, even with the British Crown taking a third.

The *Commencement,* her captain, and her crew now waited in the calm cove of an uncharted Caribbean island for that encounter.

"Well, Mr. Brossard, this being your first time as a privateer in these waters, let me explain how we work against the Spanish. You have no doubt heard that the Spanish ships come through in convoys. You see, the Spanish king maintains a very tight control over the West Indies. There are only a few legitimate open ports that treasure or merchandise can be shipped out of and only one port in Spain that all Spanish ships leave from and must return to—Seville.

"Your French privateers in past years forced the Spanish to take precautions, and now only two great fleets are organized each year to bring back the gold and silver from the New World. No longer does any treasure ship sail alone. The fleet coming from the Spanish Main, the one we are interested in, is called the *Anglice Galleon.* It is commanded by a general and usually consists of five to eight war vessels that carry forty to fifty guns each. The heavily armed thousand ton galleons usually carry most of the treasure, but not always. Many times the merchant ships, overloaded and therefore very slow, will carry some. There will be forty to fifty merchant vessels and a number of armed packet-ships. The packet-ships serve as messengers. This fleet departs from Seville sometime during the first weeks of January.

"Everything is done very much in secret. The whole fleet might stand by idly in Seville for weeks, waiting for the order to sail. When order to sail is finally given to the general commanding the fleet, he is handed three sealed packets, which contain his sailing instructions. Sealed orders are also sent by fast messenger ship in secret directly to the admiral of the West Indies at Havana, giving all the details and instructions for the treasure fleet. From the Canaries, the ships will steer a course southwest at about latitude 15° 30', catching the trade winds. The fleet usually enters the Caribbean by the channel between Tobago and Trinidad. They usually reach Cartagena about two months after sailing from Seville.

"The Admiral of Havana sends a messenger ship to Cartagena with the fleet's arrival date. The governor sends couriers with more sealed packets to the Governor of Portobelo, to the Viceroy in Lima, and to the President of Panama. These men all in turn also send more runners with more sealed packets to other towns, ports, and provinces. Word spreads that the fleet will be arriving in Cartagena, and now gold, silver, and emeralds from New Granada; gold and pearls from Margarita and Rancherias; indigo, tobacco, cocoa from Venezuela all start their overland journey by mule train to Cartagena. The merchants of Guatemala ship their gold, silver, and goods to Cartagena by way of Lake Nicaragua and the San Juan River. The South Sea armada collects the king's revenues from Lima, Bolivia, and Chile, carrying everything to Panama. The Spanish treasure ships coming from Manila also land at Panama. Everything is then carried across the high mountains and through the jungles of the isthmus by packhorse and mule train to where they will meet the *Anglice Galleons* at Portobello.

"When the treasure fleet is in the Indies, the ports at Portobello and Cartagena are closed by order of the Admiral of Havana for fear that precious information of the whereabouts of the fleet and of the value of its cargo loaded onto each ship might inopportunely leak out. This same admiral sends every warship available to guard the convoy at every point. But every Spanish ship going back to Seville from these waters must stop at Havana before its return. In Havana, the third sealed packet is opened, which gives the departure date and the course to be taken back to Seville. The ships' manifests are checked against the Governor of Cartagena's manifest, which is checked against the Viceroy's and President's manifest, and everything is counted, checked, and rechecked before sailing for Spain.

"So, Mr. Brossard, the weakness to all the Spanish plans and subterfuge is with the mandatory stop at Havana. And because of prevailing winds and currents, there is only one way for the fleet from Portobello and Cartagena to reach Havana—the Windward Passage. And the Windward Passage is where we sit, Mr. Brossard.

"And if one of my spies happens to inform me which of the merchant ships treasure was loaded aboard? Then we would have our target. But most importantly, Mr. Brossard, the Spanish officials in the Caribe don't actually mind losing a little before it reaches Cuba. You see, our piracy is actually providing the Spanish Admiral and the various Viceroys and Governors with a much-needed service. Our capture of a few Spanish ships allows these officials to steal more from the Crown. If we seize one barrel of gold, the dons claim that the pirates have taken five. We, of course, only have our one, and the corrupt officials keep four.

"In these waters, everyone is stealing from someone. When the time is right, we take our ships and attack from the shoals, cut out the merchant vessel we want, and sail back into the shallow waters where the Spanish warships can't venture because of their draft," Bill explained. "We must be fast, decisive, and quick."

The long black wig Brossard wore almost hid the dark sardonic grin that blushed across his lean, thin face for just a moment like a shadow. His necklace consisting of several green emeralds each the size of robin's eggs hung loosely from his neck as he leaned over the table, studying the map. The point of his dagger questionably stabbed at a place on the map. The fingers on the hand holding the knife were adorned with several gold rings with gems in heavy settings. This would be Brossard's first encounter with a Spanish flotilla laden with treasure. He was looking forward to the riches that would soon be his share.

"One more thing that I must caution you about, Brossard. We will undoubtedly be going up against my old friend, Admiral Don Juan Martinez de Palategui y Guzman Rocaberti. His flag ship is the *Magdalena*. It is a fast, heavily armed warship, as are the other galleons. And this man is no fool. While we may be providing him with a service by attacking his treasure convoys, it can only enhance his credibility to kill an English privateer occasionally. Also, he seems to take my stealing of Spanish treasure rather more personally than he should. Be careful of this man, Brossard. He will kill you if he gets the chance."

Master's Mate Cribb, sailing master of the *Nancy*, entered the cabin. "Mr. Cribb, can the *Nancy* be ready to sail tomorrow?" Bill asked the tall, gaunt, gray-haired captain of the sloop.

"Aye, sir. She'll be ready," Cribb replied.

Walker motioned Brossard and Cribb over to the maps on the table. "Gentlemen," he began, "here we sit with our three ships." He pointed to a place on one of the crude hand-drawn maps. "The Spanish will sail through the Windward Passage, coming from Cartagena, at about here. Our scout ships have reported thirty-five to forty vessels, and five Spanish treasure galleons make up this fleet," Bill stated as he looked for a reaction on the other two men's faces. Both were smiling.

"Now we all know that a proper British convoy would sail their ships at no farther distance than two cables apart, thereby maintaining the integrity of the fleet under the protection of their combined guns. However, these are Spanish captains," Bill emphasized, displaying his contempt for Spanish seamanship. "After eight days of sailing, by the time they reach us, they'll be spread out each a Spanish league or more away from the next. The line of ships will stretch from here to here as they come through the passage." Bill's finger traced an arc across the map. "We'll time our attack at sunset."

"And we? Where will we be?" ask Brossard.

Bill pointed to another place on the map. "The *Nancy*, posing as a small fishing vessel, will sit on the leeward side of Monkey Key, where she'll be protected and out of sight from the convoy. You and I, Mr. Brossard, will be to the west, darting between these islands, jockeying for a position that will be to our advantage. Gentlemen, we must capture this Spanish cow intact. That means without damaging her ability to sail. We will not have time to unload her cargo. We have to capture her quickly, subdue the crew, and get the ship underway before the Spanish warships regroup and attack us. Now, let's go over our plans again, gentlemen."

The discussion continued well into the night.

Prize Crew

17 July 1663, 7:00 p.m.
Off the coast of Hispaniola

Lieutenant Cribb's scarred hands rested across the heavy oak tiller as he guided the *Nancy* through the turquoise blue sea. "Steady, my lads." His calm voice resonated across the open deck, where twenty buccaneers lay hidden under tarps and fishing nets. "Steady, we'll have 'um yet, lads." The swivel guns had been removed from the gunwales and rested on the deck, also hidden under heavy canvas. Bill hoped that the men onboard the warships would believe that the *Nancy*, being so small and with the crew well hidden, was only a small fishing boat and ignore their approach.

The *Nancy* twisted and turned through the Spanish convoy of ships looking for the single merchant vessel that Cat had told Bill contained a storehouse of treasure. Cribb easily spotted the decoy that William had warned him about. The decoy was a trap. Finally, he spotted a large Spanish ship that sluggishly chopped through the water some distance to the leeward side of her armed escorts. The man at the wheel could tell as he drew nearer that the Spanish ship was heavily loaded and was sitting low in the water. It was just nearing sunset. Cribb saw the name painted in gold letters on her stern: *San Francisco de Asis.* It was the vessel that he had been looking for.

Bill, at the wheel of the *Commencement,* watched the *Nancy's* course, carefully judging distance, speed, and most importantly, estimating how much daylight remained. He also noticed that the Spanish ship Lieutenant Cribb had singled out was falling behind the rest of the fleet because she was heavily loaded and out of trim. The *Commencement* and the *Blanche Sorciere* would be coming out of the west. Both ships would be difficult for the Spanish convoy to see looking into the sunset.

The *Commencement* rounded the headland of an island jutting into the sea. "Now, Daniel!" William shouted. "Put on more sail. We'll move her into the wind. We'll have the weather gauge now, my lads. She's ours!"

The crew responded briskly, running up the ratlines to drop the sails from the spars as Bill spun the wheel, and the *Commencement* banked sharply into the wind.

"Starboard gun crews, at your ready!" William ordered. "Send the marksmen into the rigging."

The black gunports dropped open, and the bronze cannons rolled on the mahogany carriages into position.

Brossard, seeing the *Commencement* turning, banked the *Blanche Sorciere* also, and both ships now headed with the wind, bringing the Spanish vessel to a point downwind. Brossard realized an upwind vessel is able to maneuver at will toward any downwind point. This relative position is what Captain Walker had referred to as having the weather gauge. It had been the exact position that they had been trying to achieve for the better part of the day. And they had gained the weather gauge just as the sun was setting, just as Walker had planned. Now the warships and the rest of the fleet downwind must trim sail or fear being headed before attempting to fire their great guns. A heeling or headed vessel restricts the guns on the windward side of the ship because they are elevated too far upward, and the leeward side guns are pointed towards the sea.

"Port gun crews, to the ready!" Brossard ordered. "Marksmen, aloft."

As the sun set, both ships came to close quarters with the merchant. Knowing that a single broadside from the Spanish guns would sink their vessels, both captains maneuvered skillfully as to keep their bow always presented to the enemy while their musketeers cleared the galleon's deck. The chase gun on the foredeck stood at the ready. While the Spanish crew watched the two English privateers closing on both the port and starboard sides, Lieutenant Cribb was able to sail swiftly unnoticed under the galleon's stern.

After dropping the sail, Cribb quietly moved between the men. "Off with your boots, lads, so that you can climb up that sterncastle." Barefooted and armed with pistols and swords, twenty men swarmed up the sterncastle and over the deck. The helmsman was the first to die, and the Spanish ship momentarily lost steerage until Mr. Cribb had the wheel.

Fifty men onboard the *Commencement*, hanging from the rigging high above the deck, fired French seventy-caliber muskets shot with deadly accuracy onto the Spanish sailors below as William brought his vessels along side. Brossard came along the other side with the *Blanche Sorciere* with another fifty men firing muskets from the rigging. As both ships drew closer to their prey, the swivel guns, loaded with grapeshot, strafed the deck. Boarding planks and grapples were thrown across, and the crews from both ships boarded the Spanish vessel.

Not a single cannon shot had been fired. Skirmishes of pistol and musket fire came sporadically from around the ship, but within twenty minutes, the privateers had custody of the gun deck, and in a few minutes, the ship and its treasure were taken. William, along with several others, broke into the great cabin, where they threw apple-sized iron spheres packed with gunpowder and a slow-burning fuse into where the officers had barricaded themselves in a desperate last stand.

As the smoke cleared in the cabin, following the explosions, Bill saw only a single Spaniard left alive. The man seemed to be trying to set fire to a stack of papers. Bill raised his pistol as he came through the door and, mostly out of pure instinct, shot the man in the head. The burning torch the man held fell from his hand, and the papers never caught fire. The papers fell to the floor, and then the man's body fell across them.

Bill pushed the Spaniard's body aside and gathered up several volumes of what looked like, on closer inspection, nautical charts. He had no idea what they were, but if this Spaniard was trying to destroy them, then they must be something of importance. With the charts in his hands, Bill ran up the companionway that led to the weather deck.

"Mr. Brossard!" William cried as he reached the quarterdeck of the captured Spanish ship. "Mr. Brossard!"

Brossard ran toward the quarterdeck with his cutlass in hand. "Aye, Cap'n."

"Take a detail of men and secure the prisoners belowdecks," Captain Walker ordered. "Mr. Cribb!" he then shouted as Brossard moved away.

"Aye, sir," Cribb answered.

"Assemble a prize crew, Mr. Cribb. I'll leave you Big Daniel at the helm. Make fast now. The Spanish will be upon us in no time."

The dark night covered the ship by the time Brossard returned to the quarterdeck, where Walker still stood staring out across the sea.

"Can you see them, Cap'n?" Brossard anxiously asked as he too stared into the night.

"I see their lights. Just off our stern. I can't make out how many," William stated. "It'll be the smaller packet ships that we'll have to worry about. We have to get ahead of them and to our assembly point before they catch us. Pass the word to douse the lights, and no noise. Mr. Cribb will command the prize crew. You know the heading to the channel. Jagua will meet us. Even the small Spanish ships will be unable to make it through those channels in the dark. Mr. Cribb, take command," Bill said as both he and Mr. Brossard made their way back to their ships.

The *Nancy* had already pulled away from the stern of the Spanish vessel and disappeared into the night.

Within two hours, the privateer convoy had made its way to the mouth of the twisting channel that passed between shallow sandbanks and coral reefs that separated a string of rocky keys and cays that spread for miles. Each ship took its turn carefully slipping between the floating torches that marked the port and starboard sides of the channel. The *Nancy* was the last ship through the narrow passageway, and as she reached the other side, she dropped her sail and waited to see that all the rafts with the torches had been sunk and that there was nothing for the Spanish to follow.

Silently, five young girls swam to the side of the sloop and effortlessly pulled themselves out of the black water onto the deck. Once on board, they covered their naked bodies with blankets, each girl placing a coca leaf in her mouth and chewing; the euphoric pleasure of the drug washed over each of them as they caught their breath.

𝔅oucanier's Celebration

20 July 1663, 4:00 p.m.
a hidden island

All three ships and the prize vessel reached the island before sunrise. But there was no rest for Walker's men. First the ship's surgeon had to finish attending to injuries. The captured Spanish crew was interrogated to collect any useful information, and then they were loaded aboard the *Nancy* and taken to another small island, where they were set ashore, marooned. The Spanish treasure was counted and then counted again by Big Daniel the quartermaster, Adam the purser, and William the captain. After an accurate count had been determined, Adam calculated each man's share. As evening approached, Walker and Big Daniel assembled the crew and announced to all hands present what each man's share would be. Following the announcement of the division of shares, the meal that the cooks had been preparing all day was laid out for the crew. Spirits were plentiful, and each man held a bottle of rum or wine in his hand—no watered-down grog tonight.

Captain Walker gathered with Brossard and Cribb in his quarters on the *Commencement*. "My compliments and a glass of wine with you." Walker walked to the sideboard, picked up a decanter, poured Brossard and Cribb a glass of wine each, and handed it to the men. The sound of the ship's bell was heard in the cabin, where the men sat looking over the accounting of the loot from the Spanish ship.

Marcum, the captain's steward, came into the cabin. "Begging your pardon, sir, your guests are awaiting you for dinner. The crew is ashore. If you and your gentleman want a serviceable meal, then you'd best be at haste. I can't be responsible otherwise. Will has provided a feast unbounded, and the cook has everything in excellent order." Marcum had served under Captain Walker for fifteen years.

Under bright stars and a cool breeze blowing across the deck, the meal set before the captain and officers was, in fact, truly a feast beyond compare. The ship's cook was from the island of Hispaniola, a French Creole skilled at roasting and smoking wild game, fish, and turtles in the *boucan* fashion. He was a descendent from the Carib Indians who had once eaten human flesh smoked on wooden racks called barbecues over covered fires long before domestic Spanish cattle were abandoned on Hispaniola. Now, wild abandoned cattle were common throughout the Caribbean and were caught and cooked on the *boucan* by not only the local Indians but also escaped slaves seeking refuge in the islands and English and French scoundrels who cut logwood trees for a living. The French preferred calling these hunters *buucaniers* because of the way they cooked their meat and often referred to them as *flibustiers* from the word for *freebooters*, referring to their small open boats that often attacked merchant vessels at night while they lay at anchor. But later the word *filibuster* came to have a political meaning, and the Dutch term *zeeroovers* (sea rovers) was used to describe these island adventures. The Spanish called them *pyrates*. Captain Walker and his men were none of these. They were privateers commissioned by the English Admiralty as private warships under letters of reprisal and marque issued by the governor of Jamaica.

The officers gathered on deck under the white canopy for supper. Laughter and singing could be heard from the men onshore as they too enjoyed the celebration. Meals were never a time to discuss the business of the ships or the fleet; they were a social gathering that encouraged and demanded the highest courtesies being extended to fellow officers, storytelling, and good humor. Standing at the head of the table with a glass in his hand, Bill said, "A glass of wine with you each. It has been our privilege to take a few more pieces of eight away from the Spanish."

The officers stood, raised their wineglasses, and in unison replied, "And a glass of wine with you, Captain."

As the men found their places at the table and started serving their plates, Bill announced, "Gentlemen, you can be thankful for our meal tonight to Will, our Miskito Indian shipmate, and our most excellent Creole cook, Andree. Will, on his own, provided all before you, and Andree did the rest."

The ship's silver cutlery was set out, crystal goblets held dark red Spanish wine, and silver plates and bowls held the bounties of the nearby island. Andree had prepared, cooked, and served everything to perfection: delicately barbequed lime-and-pepper-sauce-marinated wild boar, roasted breast of quail garnished with mangos, steamed bananas in coconut milk, chilies, and wild rice. Thick turtle souppe was served in a silver tureen.

"Captain?" questioned Lieutenant Brossard, "is it true that one Miskito Indian can catch enough fish, turtles, wild goats, and boar in a single day to feed a ship of one hundred men?"

"Quite true, Mr. Brossard. They have been brought up from an early age to be hunters and are quite adept in the use of spears and bows and arrows. Given a little training, they made excellent marksmen with a musket. They also have extraordinary vision and can sight a sail on the horizon well before the rest of the crew."

"You know," added William Cribb, "that they are not Carib Indians, Mr. Brossard. They are *zambors*."

Outside of Lieutenant Brossard and Lieutenant William Cribb, a skilled sailing master and navigator, the other men gathered at the table were all petty officers or warrant officers. Privateer vessels didn't require layers of officers, most of whom in the Crown's Navy would have been in training, just learning their skills, and therefore useless aboard a vessel like the *Commencement*. No, the men and officers aboard this vessel were all proven seamen. Big Daniel held the position of quartermaster, Moses Adam was the purser and cartographer, Daniel Burk was the boatswain, John Littleton was the master of arms and master gunner, Doktor Jost Becker was the ship's surgeon, and Alonso Sanchez was the master carpenter.

"The *zambors* are a very unique mixed race from the coast of Nicaragua," Doktor Becker explained in a heavily accented voice. "Decades ago, a Portuguese slave ship was wrecked off the islands of Honduras. The African slaves who survived the ordeal made their way to the coast of Nicaragua and lived among the Missikis Indians. *Zambors* preferred to offer their skills to English captains. They have no love for the French and a mortal hatred for the Spanish.

Unfortunately, there are only about one hundred true *zambors* left alive today. It's a race that we will soon no longer see."

"We are fortunate then to have two *zambors* with us: Will, who spent the day hunting on the island and fishing from his heavy dugout cottonwood *pirogue*, and Lord Baltimore, who, because of his exceptional eyesight, now sits on the highest mountaintop on the windward side of the island to watch for Spanish ships coming through the passage while we lie anchored out of sight on the leeward side and enjoy this wonderful meal," said Bill.

"No salted beef and hardtack for the crew while they cruised the Caribbean," stated Alonso, laughing.

"Cap'n," requested Brossard, "if you would indulge my curiosity by answering another question? These creatures that swim in the sea like fishes, these women you call *Aycayia* women? This woman named Jagua? Where do they come from?"

"The girl called Jagua and her...let's call them her sisters, I discovered living on the beach of one of the islands, southwest of where we are now. At the time the island was called Las Mujeres del Agua, which means 'the women of the water' in Spanish. Jagua was terrified of the Spanish and feared that the Spanish would capture them and kill, rape, or enslave them as they had done the rest of her race," Bill explained. "The girls have little to do with the crew and very rarely come on board any of our ships. When they do, it's usually the open decks of the *Nancy* that they prefer. They have never gone belowdecks on any ship. Most often they swim alongside when we sail."

"Spanish journals tell of them. These journals say that they are beautiful young women who are mermaids, and they lured Spanish ships onto the rocks by their calls and singing," Brossard stated. "I have also heard that these brown-skinned beautiful girls are so vicious that the crew of Spanish ships are told that it is fatal even to think about them—these young girls would strangle and crush their victims to death."

"They be water devils," grumbled Big Daniel. "In Scotland we call them kelpie—beautiful naked woman that swims in the sea."

"It be true that scoundrels place naked tavern women on the beach to lure ships onto the rocks, but these were not the *Aycayia* women," Bill replied. "Jagua and her sisters are gentle creatures that would never strangle or crush anyone. They are certainly not water devils. They live off crabs, oysters, and I believe that I have seen them eating seaweed. I have known them to drink seawater on long voyages. However, this is not their preference."

"Mr. Brossard," Big Daniel added, "as you know, a ship on the lee shore can run upon the rocks by a change of wind, blowing as it does toward land or strong gust of wind, making a ship uncontrollable with little room to maneuver. I'm sure bad seamanship is explained by nefarious sea creatures. The Spanish are not good sailors."

"But the Greeks spoke of sirens, you know," John Littleton commented.

"So these women sea creatures, these mermaids actually exist?" Brossard asked.

Doktor Becker, listening attentively, commented, "By your own eyes they exist. And others know about them. In 1601, a Dutch naturalist caught one of these creatures in a fishing net off the coast of South America. He published his findings in a *Treatise of Brazil*. They are anatomically similar to any human woman. However, the epidermis, the skin was noted to be somewhat unusual. The sebaceous glands produced an oily serous fluid that probably protects the skin in the water. Or possibly this oil provides warmth or maybe even a defense mechanism. As we know there are some species of sea creatures that pump secretions into the water, like the ink of the squid, masking or discouraging predators. So the enlarged sweat glands or sebaceous glands may in fact provide these women with a protective cover in the water. A shark or other predators may not have ever recognized these creatures as a delightful food source because of this sebaceous oil.

"Another interesting aspect that was discovered had to do with the skin pigmentation. Melanin, as you may know, produces skin color. These creatures do not have melanin and have a relative colorless epidermis. Their skin color is produced by chromatophores in the dermis that can change color depending on the situation, like the chameleon on land or the octopus underwater. The skin adjusts to the light, and apparently, they are able to change color. On land, Jagua appears to have light brown skin with long, thick, black, oily hair hanging to the waist. In the water her translucent skin covering changes colors. I have noticed that Jagua often appears to be a dark blue when she is in the water. But by all practical measure, she appears to be human, and a beautiful human at that."

Bill poured another glass of wine and stated offhandedly, "Jagua can communicate with other sea creatures." He paused for a moment and then added, "Of this I am certain. When we sail, Jagua and her sisters follow our ships on the backs of dolphins and sometimes on the back of whales. And she can stay underwater for close to fifteen minutes. They are with us only because of the protection that we offer."

"Please excuse all my questions, gentlemen. These waters of the Caribe are new to me," stated Brossard. "Creoles, *Missikis* Indians, *zambors*, *Cimmarron* Negroes, and now naked *Aycayia* women who live in the water and follow your ships on the backs of dolphins—it's all so impossible."

"There are many more mysteries and unexplained happenings in these waters than you could ever dream of, Captain Brossard," Bill said, smiling. "Just stay alive long enough, and you will see them. Marvels beyond your imagination, lands and peoples that no one has ever encountered, horizons yet to be sailed, and riches, riches beyond even your greed. Whole cities made of gold are rumored to exist somewhere in these lands. It is said that these cities are ruled by a white tribe."

"Cities of gold? My word!" exclaimed Brossard.

"On my oath, they are said to exist. The natives speak of it. They call the city Coriancha."

While the officers dined on the deck of the ship, the crew of the three ships celebrated in a similar fashion on the white, sandy beach of the island under a canopy of lush palm fronds with the cool offshore breeze coming from the ocean as the red glow of the sun dipped into the turquoise sea at the horizon. Tonight the rum was not rationed.

As the meal ended that evening, Bill said to the men gathered at the table, "Tomorrow we return to Port Royal and divide the spoils. There'll be no more prize for us this season."

The men sat quietly around the table. No one spoke.

"Very well then, if there are no questions or further discussion, we prepare to sail tomorrow," Bill stated in a way that seemed almost absentminded. "A good season it was and a purse full of gold for all hands. Thank you, gentlemen."

Captain William Walker slept soundly that night holding Jagua's body curled next to him in his arms. Naked, she had come out of the sea after dark and up the sterncastle, through the open windows, and into Bill's cabin. Her skin was like glazed silk under his hand, and the soft oily texture of her long black smothering tangles of hair fell across him as they slept. Bill knew that she would leave. She would leave before dawn and slip out the window, down the sterncastle, and back into the sea before he even awoke. But he also knew that she would follow his ships with her sisters, and she would be back again. Back in his arms at her choosing.

The following day the *Commencement* and the captured Spanish prize vessel sailed for Port Royal. During the next two days, Bill had an opportunity to carefully examine the papers that he had taken from the dead Spaniard. He couldn't believe what he discovered. It was a prize to be sure, a prize more precious than any amount of gold or silver. Bill realized that what he had in his hands was the fabled Royal Register of maps or the *Padron Real*, which were the secret Spanish and Portuguese master maps that date back to Prince Henry. It is even said that among these maps is the original Columbus/Pinzon map that was used as a template for the maps presently carried on Spanish ships. Every Spanish ship's navigator or pilot has to be approved by first the church and then trained by the *Casa de Contratacion*, and any copies of these secret *Padron Real* ship's maps released by the *Casa* go only into the hands of the pilot. Even the ship's captain sails under sealed orders and many times never sees these maps and sometimes has no knowledge of the exact course the ship under his command will be taking.

The prize was an entire volume of Spanish charts covering the entire Caribbean with very accurate and exact descriptions of all the ports, islands, coasts, capes, creeks, and rivers, together with soundings and sailing directions on how to work a ship into every port or harbor. The information contained in the volume was of such strategic value that Bill now understood why the pilot had been ordered to destroy the set of maps before capture. Had Bill not shot the man then, the pilot would have surely set fire to the documents.

Bill wrapped the documents in a linen cloth and locked them in a sea chest sitting in his cabin. He never told anyone about this prize.

The Spanish Admiral

26 August 1663, 7:20 p.m.
Havana, Cuba

Long shadows from the buildings on the west side of Cable Obispo Street fell across the front gate of the admiral's residence as the sun dropped below the green mountaintops. The two-story villa sat inside a walled compound that spread over two city blocks, just off the town square. It was a grand residence, suitable for an admiral of nobility. And Don Juan Martinez de Palategui y Guzman Rocaberti was an admiral. In fact, he was *the* Admiral—the Spanish admiral that commanded the fleet that protected the Spanish West Indies. Had he been born in England, he might have simply been addressed as Martin. But the admiral was Spanish. And the Spanish aristocracy had their own style that embellished noble names with a grace uncommon in most other cultures. Palategui, of course, was his father's surname. It was the male branch of the family that contributed to the defeat of the Moors in 1492. The *y* indicated that whatever followed belonged to the maternal side of the family, and as all knew, the Rocaberti family were second cousins to Isabella Madrigal de las Altas Torres—Queen Isabella. Martin was the fourth son of a well-to-do Spanish family, and as a fourth son, he had limited options as to his future. He of course inherited the name, but nothing else; no property, money, or real employment fell into his hands. Therefore, only two options were open to him: the church or the military. His mother had decided that young Martin wasn't suited for the military. Therefore, at the age of twelve, the slim, dark-haired, almost frail-looking Martin entered the Order of Preachers, more commonly known as the Roman Catholic Dominican Order. His mother felt that because the Order of Preachers had been founded in 1216 by Saint Dominic de Guzman, who was a distant relative on his mother's side of the family, this would be the perfect vocation for young Martin.

The church soon recognized that Martin was exceptionally bright. Some said that the boy was gifted. In Seville, the Dominican priest filled the young boy's mind with knowledge. He quickly learned several languages, history, geography, mathematics, the church's version of astronomy and science, and most importantly, he learned that the church had a moral right to impose whatever punishment necessary to combat heresy, wherever it might be found and in whatever form it might take. The friars and bishops of the church also learned that young Martin had other distinctive qualities that some members inside a very exclusive order were looking for. The boy, they discovered, was not only bright; he was also cunning, devious, and cruel. Martin, at the age of fifteen, was initiated into the Order of the Black Friars and wore the ominous black *cappa*. He was the youngest novice, or in the Latin that most in the order spoke, he was the youngest *apperendere* ever to wear the black robe of the Inquisition. During his time at the monastery, the church had censored many books and writings in an effort to impede the diffusion of heretical ideas. But his membership in this order gave him very special access into the "indexes" of prohibited documents that others could never hope to see.

Inside the cloisters of the Dominican monastery, Martin studied these forbidden text for fifteen years. The boy was, by all accounts, an exemplary and gifted student, and he willing embraced the values of this secret order that had been established to prevent Jewish *conversos*, Protestants, and *Moriscos* from contaminating the pure values of Spain and the Catholic Church. But Martin soon began to wonder if the order really served God or only itself and the monarchy. The Inquisitor General, in charge of the Holy Office, was appointed by the King of Spain and was the only public office whose authority stretched to all kingdoms of Spain, including the Caribbean.

At the age of twenty-five, Martin unexpectedly left the church. No one knew why he had suddenly made this choice, but after leaving the church, he used his family's influences to gain a position as an officer in the Spanish Navy. Rank within the Spanish Navy came easily to Martin because it was not predicated on knowledge of seamanship or experience. Advancements were haphazardly based on who your family was and how they catered to the court and king. After gaining his commission, his mother enhanced his standing even further with bribes to government officials and by an arranged marriage to a thirteen-year-old girl named Agueda, the only daughter of Bartolome Gomez y Ana de Torres, who was a favorite at the Spanish Court. Martin obtained what he was looking for—a position in the Caribbean. It had taken him five years and more bribes to gain the office of admiral. But he knew that at any price, it would be worth it.

Now after eight years in the Caribbean, Martin lived in the grand home just down the street from the Plaza on Cable Obispo and had more power than the Governor General of Cuba or any other Governor or Viceroy in any province of the Spanish Indies and wheedled it unmercifully for his own interest and the interest of his family. "My Spain against all countries, my religion against all other religions, my family against all other families, and my wife and children against my brother's wife and children," he would often remind himself. Admiral de Palategui was responsible for safeguarding the convoys of treasure ships as well as the cities and the ports where any treasure might be amassed. His every order was carried out without question because Don Juan Martinez de Palategui y Guzman Rocaberti controlled the navy, soldiers, and all the Spanish ships coming to and leaving the Caribbean.

With his young wife and family safeguarding his interest in the Court of Spain, Martin spent his time and energies stealing as much as decency would allow and finding lucrative jobs for family members, discreetly inserting them into positions in the Caribe that would not only secure and enrich his relatives but would also support his own plans for the future of his family.

Martin knew that Spain's foreign policy in the Indies had been wretchedly and notoriously corrupt from the very beginning. It was split between three factions, each suspicious of the other, one plotting against the next, and each trying to steal as much as possible. On the one hand, there was the powerfully endowed church that filled the colonies with thousands of idle, unproductive, and often licentiously greedy friars who had first traveled, by mandate of the church, beside the conquistadors. Unfortunately, these monks were the only ones that could either write or read, Spanish aristocracy at the time seeing no value in either, and therefore, all the records of discovery in the New World were written mostly by Dominican friars. Then there was the privileged nobility who had a disdain for any manual labor or hard work that lived on the huge country estancias granted by the Crown of Spain to families favored at court. They either enslaved the local natives and raised sugarcane or imported cattle. Cattle were not indigenous to the Americas; they came from Spain. The dry climate with sparse grass was similar to Spain, and the *hacienda* system of large herds covering vast amounts of land in order to obtain sufficient forage was adopted. *Vaqueros* riding Andalusian horses also came from Spain. And finally, there was the civil administration that only lived in the larger cities, all of whom from the lowest public official right up to the governors and viceroys had bribed their way into these lucrative positions, hoping to quickly amass their fortune and then return to Spain as soon as possible.

But Martin had a vision for himself and his family that was quite different from the other corrupt officials around him. Even though Don Agustin de Bracamonte, his cousin on his wife's side, commanded Panama, and Captain Castellan Alexandro Manuel Pau y Rocaberti commanded Portobello, and the viceroy of Cartagena, another rich Spanish port, was also a family member, and he could therefore steal as much as he wanted, his ambition didn't rest with simple greed. No, Martin had read histories and seen documents in the monastery where he had studied for years that led him toward a much different goal. And after leaving the church, he spent every day planning just how he would achieve what he felt was his moral destiny. He vowed that nothing would stand in his way, and under the guise of the Inquisition, he burnt, hung, or savagely dismembered any who might pose a threat or interfere with his plans.

Martin wanted more than just gold. Martin saw himself as an emperor. An emperor in a fashion much like the Roman emperors he had read about, an emperor of his own sovereign country in the New World. He saw himself as not only a king in this new land but a king chosen by God who would had divine privileges over his kingdom.

A dark Gypsy girl with long black hair named Catlina was said to be his only weakness. At twenty-two years old, Catlina stood a mere five foot eight inches tall. Her long, curly, black hair hung to her waist, and her full, heavy, firm breasts stood erect under the light blue cotton camisole that she wore. A bright red, pleated, light cotton skirt pulled salaciously up in the front and pinned to the wide leather black belt at her waist revealed scant glimpses of her brown thighs while black boots coming almost to her knees hugged the meaty calves of her legs. Cat was one of the troupe of Gypsy dancers and musicians that routinely performed for the Admiral of Cuba and his guests inside the extensive naval fortification that protected Havana's harbor. She was, in fact, Martin's mistress and his only weakness.

"De Leon, Pizarro, and Francisco de Orellana all wrote in their journals about this city! A city of gold called Coriancha!" Martin exclaimed to Catlina, who sat salaciously sprawled across the couch in Martin's study. One of her bare legs dangled over the raised end of the leather settee as she curiously watched Martin pace the red clay tile floor in front of the large map that had been meticulously painted across one entire wall. The other brown leg rested on the floor, her skirt pulled back to her thighs.

"De Orellana, the bastard, probably even saw the city but never told Pizarro the location, hoping to keep everything for himself. They were no less corrupt in those days than they are today, and none of these records are complete!" he shouted, throwing a leather-bound journal across the room in frustration. "No, nothing is complete. I've read their journals, the uncensored ones, the secret manuscripts that only came to the church. But even these have somehow been censured by those stupid priests. So even if Francisco had noted the discovery, it might have been omitted. But the registry at the Abbey of Santiago might hold the key that I'm looking for."

Santiago de Cuba was one of the oldest cities in the Spanish Caribbean. During its time, the city was more important than any in Hispaniola. It had been built years before Havana in 1514, and its deepwater bay was where the first conquistadors sailed from to explore the New World and, more importantly, where they came back to before returning to Spain. It was the starting point for all the expeditions. Juan de Grijalba and Herman Cortes started there to explore the coast of Mexico. It was from Santiago that Herman de Soto's ships left to explore Florida. Santiago had been the first center of Spanish power in the Indies. So Santiago Abbey, Martin speculated, was where the majority of the old uncensored documents, records, and possibly even maps might still be found.

"I must get to Santiago!"

"But why is this city in the jungle so important, my dear?" Catlina asked in a soothing, gentle voice. "You have gold. More gold than either you or your family for generations to come could ever spend. And you have power, which, for some men, is more important than gold. What is a city of gold more or less to a man that has everything?"

Standing in front of the large colorful fresco map that spread across one entire wall, Martin seemed to ignore her question and pointed to a blank section. "Up here along one of these rivers is where it has to be. It has to be along here somewhere. But which river?" And the slim brown palm of his right hand covered a place on the map. "It's there in Portuguese lands. Coriancha is there, of that I am certain," Martin stated as there was a knock on the door.

"Entrada!" said the admiral in a soft voice, and a short brown Indian woman with shiny raven-black hair that hung below her shoulders and cut severely in a line just above her dark eyebrows entered the room. She was dressed in a white blouse and a faded red pleated skirt that hung just below her knees, where slim brown legs ended in worn leather sandals that covered her wide calloused feet. "Captain Silva is outside, Excellency," the girl said respectfully.

"Please show him in, Tz'iken," Martin said.

Catlina knew that the woman's name was from the ancient Aztec language Akateko that many natives still spoke. Translated, the name meant "bird," which the young woman certainly resembled.

Catlina moved to the side of the room as Captain Eduardo Santos Tavares Melo Silva entered the admiral's study.

Captain Silva pushed his way roughly past Tz'iken. As he entered the room, he noticed the double set of wide French doors opening onto a shaded garden courtyard, and from somewhere beyond the steamy warmth that wrapped itself in the evenings around the town of Havana, a cool breeze flowed through the open doors into the room where the man he hated sat behind a desk. White lace curtains drifted in the gentle breeze like soft billowing sails. But more than the breeze, the room's coolness seemed to come from the tall, slender, dark-eyed man who sat behind the desk in the middle of the room. From his burnished complexion, Silva could clearly see that the man was of Spanish noble descent. A thin mustache traced the man's upper lip. The man behind the desk didn't smile in his direction, and only a momentary flicker of his cold black eyes toward Silva directed him toward a chair.

"Eduardo, what information do you have for me today?" Martin said lightly in greeting to the Portuguese mercenary. "A glass?"

Silva couldn't meet the other man's intense cold stare and instead found himself staring for a brief moment out the window at the town's church steeple. His right hand unconsciously moved to cross himself. Then following the fluid movements of the Gypsy girl coming across the room he smiled. "Just a rumor that I picked up from an old sailor in Curacao," he said almost whimsically.

Catlina handed him a glass of wine and moved away quickly.

"Thank you, my dear," he muttered in a choked voice as a sinful leer crossed his face. Cat, seeing the look on the man's face, was repulsed and walked quickly to the back of the room.

"Then we need only to discuss your price."

"Three hundred pesos, Your Excellency," Eduardo whispered as he looked up, glancing briefly into this man's cold eyes. "Three hundred pesos," he said again louder, in a voice as confident as he could muster. Looking into this man's eyes, he was suddenly afraid and wanted nothing more than to be done with this deal, no matter what the price. He wanted just to leave. He was afraid.

Silva was a slave trader. Slave traders in the Indies were by nature brutal men, and the Portuguese were the worst of the lot. Silva feared no one, no one but this man who sat before him.

"Three hundred pesos! Silva, is this information worth that much?"

"Yes, Your Excellency," Silva said, taking a drink of the wine and swallowing the dry lump in his throat. "The old sailor that I spoke of is alive and says that he has been to the Temple of the Sun, Coriancha. In fact, he said that he lived there for years."

"Tell me what you know."

Silva slowly began to unravel his story as Cat periodically filled his glass.

"As a young boy, this sailor was aboard a Portuguese vessel that wrecked somewhere off the coast of South America. After the disaster, he made shore with most of the crew, but as they crawled onto the beach, he told me that they were attacked by natives who killed everyone except him. These natives were cannibals," he added. "Wounded and left for dead, the boy managed to escape into the jungle while the savages roasted the living survivors over open pits. For weeks he wandered deeper and deeper into the forest, always fearing for his life. Finally, dying from his wounds and fever, he collapsed, only to be found by a native girl, who nursed him back to health. She took him back into the jungle where she lived.

"As he regained his strength under her care, they fell in love, and eventually, they understood each other's language. In the years that followed, she showed him vast treasures that were far beyond his imagination that were hidden in a city deep in the jungle. After years of living in this golden city around marvelous treasures, he longed for home and persuaded the girl to go back with him to England, where he promised her that she would be clothed in silks, a fabric that the girl had never known, and they would always be together, and he would always love her and take care of her. The girl agreed to go with him, and she helped him.

"Together they secretly constructed a raft outside the golden city to carry a small part of the treasure down the river to the sea. The boy, who was now a man full grown, made a kind of crude map on their voyage down the river. He could neither read nor write, and without a compass or any means of navigation and no real knowledge of mapmaking, he drew pictures of landmarks that he hoped would guide him back to the city. It was a whole series of charcoal drawings, starting at the city from where they left and ending at the mouth of the river along the coast.

"The trip downriver was not without its perils, and just as they were approaching the ocean, the raft overturned. All the treasures spilled into the river. With crocodiles infesting the water, the two lovers barely made it to shore alive, and of course, there was no hope of recovering any of the treasure. At the coast they finally managed to signal a European ship to rescue them. The native girl and the sailor ended up in Curacao. But when I talked to him, he was an old man, barely alive. He was impoverished, penniless, and without means, drinking in a bar. But, Excellency, the girl, the same girl who had found him in the jungle when he was but a lad, still looked to be no more than seventeen or eighteen years old—she had not aged."

"But this girl could have been his daughter. Could she not?" questioned Martin.

"Maybe," Silva answered. "But I swear on God's cross, she is not his daughter."

"And where is this old man now?" asked Martin.

"He's safe. I have him."

"And the girl?" asked Martin.

"I don't know, Your Excellency," Silva lied. He had actually taken the girl to Port Royal, where she was hidden in a church under the care of a priest.

Eduardo was feeling more confident now, and a thin smile crossed his lips. *I have this sailor. I have the girl, and I have the drawings*, he thought to himself.

"And what do you plan to do?"

"Your Excellency, I am only your servant. I plan to do nothing. I'm just a messenger. But I think that three hundred pesos for this information is a fare price. And then if you want this sailor or the maps, we can negotiate a price."

Martin thought for a moment before answering. "Very well, Eduardo. The three hundred pesos are yours. You have done well. Catlina, bring Captain Silva another glass of wine," he commanded.

A greedy smile briefly crossed Silva's face as he took the drink from Catlina's hand. "But before I go any further, I want some proof," the admiral stated. "What can you show me? Where is evidence that this is not just another story told by some drunken sailor? Show me something, Eduardo. Please, show me something that supports this wild tale."

Catlina watched as Silva carefully removed several sheets of old-looking brown paper from the inside pocket of his long coat. She could see that the papers were filled with faint black drawings. Silva handed the papers to Martin.

After a few minutes, a frown crossed the admiral's face. "They are pretty drawings, but worthless!" he shouted. "Worthless! This could be anywhere!"

"But it is something, Your Excellency," Silva said as there was a knock on the door.

A Contrabano Ship

18 September 1663, 9:45 a.m.
the Blue Goat, Port Royal

Captain Walker made his way from the *Commencement* anchored in Chocolate Hole into the hidden grotto that connected to the subterranean, honeycomb of limestone caves and tunnels running under Port Royal. Drifting silently into a place called Sharks Grotto, he beached the *Commencement*'s skiff inside the dark cavern, lit the torch he had brought with him, and walked through the branching tunnel that he knew ran under the fish market under Lime Street and finally into the storage cellar of the Blue Goat. Bill had taken residence at the Blue Goat Inn soon after arriving in Jamaica with Admiral Penn in '55. But of course back then it had been a Spanish tavern. He knew the people, and he knew the secrets of the island, the cave system running under Port Royal being one of those well-kept secrets.

He pushed the large empty rum barrel aside and entered the familiar underground storage cellar of the Blue Goat. The torch extinguished, he walked out of the cellar and into the back door of the pub, where he parted the beaded curtains and entered the short hallway that led into the building. Walking past the stairs leading to his room upstairs, Helen greeted him. Taking his hand, she kissed him warmly. "I've a new girl for you," she said slyly as she held his hand and led him to a table. "She's a virgin just off the prison ship that came in yesterday. I was saving her for you."

The Blue Goat was just one of many taverns, inns, and brothels that operated in Port Royal, which, by the sixteen hundreds, had earned the reputation as the "wickedest city in Christendom." A two-story granite stone building, the tavern sat on the corner of Lime and James Streets. Lime Street was a muddy cobblestone path that ran from the harbor, lined with wharves, storehouses, warehouses, and sail lofts, past the Anglican church, past one of the two prisons, several markets, and dozens of shops. High Street was really the main thoroughfare; starting at North Docks, it ran down the center of the city, past the governor's mansion, the Admiralty Court and the Customs House, and everything from taverns and inns to blacksmiths and apothecaries. James Street was little more than an alley that connected High Street with Lime Street. Though the town had expanded in the decade of British rule, the local sewer system was unable to cope, and the open trenches that ran beside the cobblestone streets gave the air outside the Blue Goat a distinct odor.

The city had been built on top of a rock composed of calcium carbonate, a sort of blend of crystalline calcite and carbonate mud, produced by calcium-secreting coral from ancient seabeds. The coral formed layer after layer of this carbonate mud, which, over centuries, was compacted into limestone on top of the older igneous, metamorphic rock that sat on the tectonic plates of the ocean's floor. The immense weight of the limestone created heat, causing the tectonic plates of the seabed to expand and shift under the pressure. Volcanoes erupted to relieve the pressure and the heat from under the earth's thin crust. Over time, the 4,411-square-mile white-limestone island of Jamaica lifted out of the sea, and molten lava spilled from the volcanic mountains that dominated the landscape, running east to west down the center of the island. As deep volcanic soil covered the land, thick tropical foliage, fed by abundant gentle rains, sprouted from the rich earth. Royal palms, coconut trees, orchids, flaming poinsettias, hibiscus, and banyan trees covered the island. Underground, a labyrinth of caverns, tunnels, caves, and grottos with stalactite and stalagmite formations, huge calcite pillars, and deep subterranean crystal clear black lakes were carved out of the white-limestone foundation as rainwater chiseled its way down through the porous rock to find the sea. White coral sands formed along the shoreline, and waves broke through the towering limestone cliffs to form grottos that connected the sea to the underground caverns. Openings to the surface, now hidden inside the town of Port Royal, and sinkholes provided some ventilation but also collected sewage from above, and some of the underground caverns smelled as bad as the city. The caves were first used by Tainos Indians. The Spanish had kept their existence secret, and few British now living in Port Royal had any idea that there were caves just below their feet. Smugglers and privateers knew the hidden openings to this subterranean world, and they used the caverns as meeting and hiding places.

The ground floor of the Blue Goat was dedicated to drinking, gambling, and dining. The upper floor was divided into small bedrooms. Off the left side of the building separated from the main dwelling due to the heat from hot wood fires that burned in open brick pits and ovens was the cookhouse, where meals were prepared for the guest. There was really nothing like a door at the back of the tavern, just an opening with a beaded curtain that brushed aside as sailors tried to make their way to a single unpainted wood privy that sat some distance away from the building. A white-roofed underground cellar sat off to the right as you walked to the privy. Kegs of rum, casks of brandy, and wine were stored in the cool, dark limestone cellar. Behind one of the walls where large rum kegs had been stacked was concealed the hidden passageway that Bill had come through.

When rum was brought to the table, Bill asked Helen, "The Persian and Adam, where are they?"

The Persian was a Muslim, a Saracens. He had once been a galley slave chained to the oars of a Barbary Coast pirate vessel in the Mediterranean. When Bill captured the vessel years ago, he freed the Persian and the other slaves from their chains before setting fire to the renegade ship. Since his freedom, the Persian had followed Bill everywhere. As Bill was to discover over the years of their companionship, the Persian was a very educated, highly intelligent individual. He was well versed in the sciences, engineering, mathematics, philosophy, and chemistry.

"Adam is in the next room. I don't know about the Persian, Bill. The fellow doesn't drink and is particular about his women. So he's sober, and if chance favored him last night, he's probably with one of the Negro or Arab women, somewhere farther down the dock where those kinds of women are available. Maybe Adam knows," she said.

Bill glanced around the room. Sure enough, sitting at a corner table in the shadows sat Adam, the ship's purser. Bill walked casually to the table where Adam was drinking his coffee. Bill had never known Adam to drink anything stronger than coffee.

Moses Adam was of medium height with a dark complexion. His long gray hair was pulled back in a loose ponytail. He fashioned a heavy brown mustache, which was accompanied by long, bushy gray sideburns that extended down his square jaw. Adam was an artist, a painter, a cartographer, a calligrapher. As a young man, he had been a Jewish *sofer*, a scribe, who had faithfully created hand-drawn copies of the Torah in stylish Hebrew and Aramaic calligraphy. Using these writing skills, he had been employed as a clerk by lawyers, government ministers, and judges over the years. But Adam had wanderlust so common to young men of this age. He wanted to travel and see the world. So he had joined the British Navy first as a purser, but he found and the British Navy discovered that his real skill, his talent, was in cartography—mapmaking.

"Adam, any messages?" asked Bill as he approached the table.

"Aye, Cap'n." Adam dug into his purser's bag and withdrew several sheets of paper of various sizes and handed them to Bill. "This one came in yesterday, these came in a few days ago, this one two weeks past," stated Adam.

"Thank ye, Adam." Bill took the messages and shuffled through the first few. Adam was the perfect covert courier. As a ship's purser, he carried, sent, and received messages every day. His bag was full of invoices, bills of laden, written request, letters, and assorted documents. A message delivered to or discovered on Adam would bring no undue attention. Adam many times used homing pigeons to receive messages. Another idea of the Persians, who had caught wild rock pigeons and trained them to return to Port Royal. These birds could travel five hundred miles or more in a single day at speeds of fifty knots or better.

Glancing at the messages that Adam had given him, two caught his attention. One was a secret note from Cat (Catlina Montoya) in Havana. The other was a letter from his father in England. He lit the candle on the table and passed what appeared to be a simple bill of laden across the heat of the flame, which revealed hidden brown writing on the back of the paper. "Come to me. What you seek is behind a great iron door," it read.

"Have you seen the Persian?" asked Bill.

"He'll be at Chin's Apothecary, studying his chemicals, or at Walla's, the gunpowder merchant," Adam said.

Both Chin's and Walla's establishments were located a block south of the Blue Goat on New Street. Bill found the Persian at the apothecary. Both Chin and the Persian seemed to be in a deep discussion about some chemical mixture or substance as Bill entered the shop.

"Salaam," Bill said to the Persian, who stood and bowed, putting his hand first to his forehead and then to his heart.

"Cap'n, peace be with you as well," the Persian greeted him.

Bill closed the door behind him. "Ahmed." Bill bowed. "May the blessings of Allah be upon you." Then turning to the Chinese gentleman, Bill said, "Master Chin, good day to you, sir. My friends, I believe I may need your help once again."

Chin showed William and Ahmed to a table located toward the back of the store behind a silk curtain, and bringing tea to the table, he also sat down with the other two men.

"How can I get through an iron door?" Bill put the question to both men.

"How thick is this door? Is it tempered steel or iron?" asked the Persian.

"Is it encased in wood or stone? What do you know of the lock? How is it held?" asked Chin.

"I would guess that it's encased in a stone doorframe. I don't know the thickness, and I don't know about the locking mechanism. But I would imagine that it is the most secure that the Spanish are able to build on land," Bill replied.

Chin and the Persian discussed the problem between themselves for a few moments. Chin then gathered a quill, a bottle of ink, and some paper, and the two men sat at the table drawing sketches of doors, hinges, and locks, playing with some mathematical notations, and discussed the problem further.

Finally the Persian said, "The fastest, simplest way to breach an iron door is to use explosives. We could use black powder which is a mixture of 10% sulphur, 15% wood charcoal and 75% potash if you just want an explosion. If you want a fire as well as an explosion, I can add another chemical. Two kegs, fifty pounds, would be needed."

"I don't believe that the Spanish will let me carry two kegs of gunpowder into Havana to blow the door off of the admiral's safe," said Bill, laughing. "No, I'll need something else. Something less crude and easily carried by one man."

The three men sat silently at the table while Chin and the Persian pondered Bill's response. The Persian then said, "The weakest point of a door is either at the hinges where the door is attached to the frame or at the lock. The weight of the iron door might actually help us because the hinges have to bear that weight and also hold it onto the stone frame. The bolt or the locking mechanism might extend completely across the door or extend several feet into the stone wall. So the hinges would be the weakest point and what we need to examine. We could use an acid, a corrosive to eat through the iron, but that might take days of repeated application. No, explosives have to be the answer, and some way to concentrate the explosion to the hinges," said the Persian.

"You can't do that with black powder," commented Chin sternly.

They sat in silence again for a few more moments.

"I may know of something. Come back later, and we'll see," the Persian said.

"Rum!" Bill demanded as he entered the front door of the Blue Goat. Helen led him to a table and put a green onion-shaped bottle of Kill Devil she held in her hand in front of him. Three glasses seemed to materialize out of nowhere, and she sat the glasses on the table also. Helen then took a chair across the table from Bill and poured out two glasses of amber liquor from the green bottle. "You need a drink, Bill," she said softly.

"That I do, my dear woman. That I do."

"Will you be staying with us tonight?" Helen asked coyly with a wide smile. "Or will you be going back to your ship?"

"I will stay here if you will share a glass with me. And then your bed later tonight."

"And how could any woman decline such an offer? But as I said, I have something more exciting for you. The new girl! Remember?" Helen kissed Bill and left the table. She returned in a few minutes with a frightened girl. The girl was young, pretty, and bawdy. She wore a long, tight-fitting, red gown that revealed every curve of her body. Loose, wanton, curling dark hair hung to her bare shoulders. She giggled as Helen placed her in a chair next to Bill and poured both the girl and William a drink.

"Captain Walker, may I introduce Monique," Helen said in a formal fashion.

One of the girl's hands gasped the glass of brown liquid, and she took a long drink. The other hand moved under the table to grope Bill's leg.

Helen smiled and, with a parting "Enjoy!" left the table.

Ignoring the girl, Bill blissfully drank one pewter tankard of Kill Devil after another. He gulped down mouthfuls of the strong liquor. Each swallow seemed to purge his soul as the alcohol meandered its way to his brain, and looking at the young prostitute that sat silently before him, he thought about Catlina. "Damn them all," he said under his breath. "Damn them all."

As the hours of the evening passed, the frightened girl started to cry. "I don't please you, my lord?" she whimpered tearfully as Bill, ignoring her, took another drink.

Helen came across the room to where the captain and the young girl sat. She pushed the crying whore aside. "Go to your room," she commanded sternly. "I'll see to the Cap'n."

As the girl left the table, Helen sat down next to William. "Well, Cap'n?" she questioned as she pulled his head back and kissed him. "You've had your cup and then some, I'd say. And you don't fancy the new wench, Cap'n?" She laughed as she pulled his shirt open and ran her hand across his chest. "Come upstairs with me."

"A glass with you, my dear," Bill whispered to Helen as he took her into his arms. "More rum!" he then shouted to the crowd. "More rum and a fling with a dandy woman."

The mob of seamen in the tavern responded to the shout with laughter, profanities, and encouragement.

"Take her, Cap'n!" one man shouted.

"Rum and plunder!" another sailor in the crowd screamed.

Helen slipped her blouse from her shoulders and pulled it down to her waist. Her large, plump bare breasts stood erect. Then she hiked her skirt up, revealing pale-white thighs, and sat in Bill's lap.

In the early hours of the next morning, the smoke-filled tavern was dark as Bill lifted his head from against Helen's cool white breasts and glanced around the room. The few oil lamps that lit the interior had burned dry, and no one had bothered to refill them. Dawn was approaching. Bill slumped over the table while Helen held him. Back against one wall stood a solitary man richly dressed in a long blue cloak covering a white ruffled silk shirt and maroon britches. A wide-brimmed beaver hat sat firmly on his head, covering a long curly-haired brown wig. The man had a tough, weathered dark face with a deep white scar, almost a welt, which ran from his forehead to his chin and then disappeared into a black beard that covered his neck and then spread onto his chest. His limp, watery blue eyes peered from under the hat and were fixed on Bill. He stood gracefully with the dignity of a gentleman and walked casually toward where Bill was still holding Helen in his arms.

As the man approached the table, he shouted, "Walker, you bastard! God shames the devil for your sins." The jeweled, silver-ringed fingers of the man's hand rested on the gold hilt of a cutlass that protruded from a wide leather belt around his fat stomach.

"Chevalier du Plessis, you French bastard!" Bill yelled back, laughing as he stood, holding Helen for support. To all eyes in the tavern, Bill was apparently drunk. But unseen, Bill's left hand moved to grasp the thirteen-inch double-edged thrusting dagger hidden at the center of his spine under his coat. Holding Helen aside, he embraced Chevalier with one arm and with the other hand thrust the hidden dagger straight through the man's black beard to where it just touched the Frenchman's throat. The knife just pierced the skin at Chevalier's neck, and blood fell onto the front of the man's lacy white shirt.

"The devils own you, bastard. Do you come here eager to kill me, Chevalier?" Bill quietly whispered into the man's ear as he pushed the point of the dagger even deeper into the man's throat.

"No, Bill. No," he pleaded. "You have me wrong. I don't set against you or any other." Several tough-looking sailors, apparently part of Chevalier's crew, rushed forward, drawing swords and long knives.

"Cap'n!" Helen protested, stepping between the two men and pushing each apart. "Cap'n," her soft voice pleaded calmly. "Come with me, I take you to my bed. Leave this man alone. There'll be no killing tonight in my establishment!"

"No. No killing tonight. I think that Captain Chevalier and I might have a word. And a glass together," Bill stated as he withdrew the dagger from the Frenchman's throat. The other men, Chevalier's crew, that had gathered around rested their weapons and returned to their tables as Bill and Chevalier both peacefully sat down.

Helen held Bill at her side tentatively while the men talked. She still expected that Bill would kill the Frenchman. There was bad blood between them. Helen had been there the night that Bill and Chevalier had come to odds, and Bill had scarred his face in a knife fight.

"Are you still running contraband out of Cuba, Chevalier?" Bill asked.

Helen pulled Bill closer and kissed him.

"Occasionally. Why do you ask?" answered the Frenchman.

Catlina

2 October 1663, 1:30 p.m.
Havana, Cuba

Bill could see the smoke coming from the Gypsy campfires as he followed his Romani guide to the top of the mountains that overlooked San Cristobal de la Habana. From Port Royal, Bill sailed with Chevalier aboard his *contrabando* ship that was headed for Cuba to pick up black market cargo. The ship landed along a secluded coast on the southern shore of Cuba in the Bay of Batabano at 22° 48' north latitude. The captain of the *contrabando* vessel called the place Melena, but there was nothing much there except a few thatched huts, fishing nets drying in the sun, and small wooden boats pulled onto the beach—just a typical fishing village. Amaya, his guide, had been waiting in the village with two horses when Bill arrived. Together they began the two-day journey across Cuba to the Port of Havana and the Gypsy camp that was just outside the city.

Amaya was a Romani, a Gypsy from Cadiz, as were the other members of his tribe now camped outside Havana, who had fled the cruelties of the Spanish Inquisition and King Philip's harsh laws that persecuted the entire Romani race in Spain. Unfortunately, the Catholic Church and finally the Inquisition had followed the Spanish colonies to the New World. The Tribunal del Santo Oficio de la Inquisicion had been established in Cartagena two years ago to administer the church's wishes concerning Jews, Persians, Gypsies, and generally anyone else that was not Spanish Catholic in the Caribbean. So Amaya and his tribe still had to be careful of outsiders and still faced indiscriminate persecution, even in Cuba.

But their unique skills made them valuable in the New World, and therefore, the various Gypsy tribes and their camps were tolerated to a large extent. Different tribes had different skills. The Argintari were silversmiths, the Aurari were goldsmiths, the Ungaritza were blacksmiths that specialized in bladed weapons, and the Gabori were jewelers. Amaya was from the Gatanos clan. The Gatanos men were horse and animal trainers, and the women were dancers and fortune-tellers. The whole tribe seemed to be gifted musicians. Like the camp followers, who were the original Gypsies, that had traveled behind Alexander the Great's vast armies, providing the necessary skills and services his army required as he conquered the known world, Amaya was an ethnic mixture of Persian, Greek, Spanish, Indian, and Arabic cultures. He spoke only *Calo*, which is a form of Andalusian Spanish that Bill was not familiar with.

William had met Catlina Montoya years before. Cat and her father, Diego, had always provided Bill with reliable information over the years about Spanish shipping—their cargos, their destinations, their sailing and arrival dates, and what kind of and numbers of naval escorts that might be sent alongside as protection. Cat's tribe moved on whatever ship was available throughout the Spanish Main to the various towns and coastal ports, applying their trade; they went everywhere, unnoticed by everyone. They were vagabond performers, show people with trained bears and horses, dark-skinned, bright-eyed girls in pleated skirts with low-cut blouses who danced to the twelve-beat pulse of a classical blend of Indian, Arabic, and Persian music. The melody of the guitars, reminiscent of the Arabic *oud*, and the slow resonating strings of violins was accentuated by the *palmas*, a staccato hand clapping, and the intermittent, punctuated voices of women singing, individually on their turn "the cante" in deep, low-pitched-baritone, throaty voices. The women's songs were in sycophantic rhythm to the twelve-beat pace and the hollow sound of the dancers' high-heeled boots prancing on the hardwood floors. The sounds of their music, voices, and heels pierced the still night wherever they gathered.

Bill followed Amaya into the Gypsy camp. Even though this campsite was somewhat permanent and the tribe had lived in this same place for months, brightly painted Gypsy wagons still dominated the landscape, and outside of stabling for the horses and a steel cage for two trained black bears, there were no structures that weren't on wheels and could not be moved at a moment's notice. It was the Gypsy life. The men wore colorful puffed-sleeved calico shirts with heavy, loose-fitting dark riding britches laced with leather thongs below the knees and tall black leather boots. Large-brimmed black hats covered their long dark hair. Some wore bright scarves around their necks. Others had long, wide red sashes tied at the waist. Their attire suited their profession of horse trainers.

The women all wore pleated layered skirts hiked up in the front above their knees, revealing tall high-heeled, laced leather boots suitable for dancing. Bright chiffon, calico, and metallic fibers seemed to be the preference. Cat had told Bill that a Gypsy never wore white because the color white was associated with death. Most women wore colorful puffed-sleeved linen blouses with very low necklines, showing ample bosoms vicariously pushed up from below by a bustier or corset that was laced firmly on top of the blouse. Layers of jewelry and gold coins adorned their necks and were sometimes sewn into the fabric of the skirts or blouses. Large gold-and-silver hooped earrings dangled to their shoulders. If married, a Gypsy girl must display that fact by keeping her long dark hair covered by a *diklo*—a headscarf. Unmarried women sometimes braided jewelry and gold coins into their long hair as a sign of their wealth and their availability.

"My friend of the *bori lon pani*, the great *tiffi*!" (My friend of the Great Salt Water, the ocean, the great sailor) shouted Diego, the chief of this clan, as Bill and Amaya rode into the camp.

Climbing from his horse, Bill embraced the tribal chief in the Gypsy fashion, and they both walked to one of the campfires, where Bill was offered a small wooden stool. A woman poured him a cup of wine in a silver chalice. Diego sat next to him by the fire, and the woman poured him wine in a matching silver chalice.

"My good friend Diego, thank you for the warm greeting and friendship in your camp. Is your wife as beautiful as ever? Your *chikinis* [daughters], are they well? And are you still a rich man?" Bill asked.

"My wife has been fat since a year after I married her, and she gets fatter each day. She is no longer the handsome woman that I married!" he exclaimed, laughing. "But she is comfortable. My daughters are *objus*. Four are married, as you know, two are dancers, but I still have one that is ten years old and another that is twelve. Both are very *objus* [beautiful] girls and dance! You must see them dance, my friend. It is magnificent. They are my life, and I must consider Francisca's destiny soon. She is a *chavi*, a young girl of twelve, and it's time for us to think about her future," Diego said.

Bill knew that in this closed Gypsy society, women never married non-Roma men and, that in a culture that survived on offering music and women dancers to outsiders as well as other cardinal pleasures, a girl's virginity was essential in marriage within the Roma culture. Therefore, fathers had to consider where their own wealth and their daughter's future might best lay, a marriage at the young age of twelve or thirteen years old, to assure virginity, to a man within the tribe or to groom his daughter to be a *looverni*, a courtesan, a prostitute. Like their distant Arab ancestors of the *Ouled Nail* tribe, women were never forced or expected to practice harlotry; it was by choice. If they took this path, young girls started learning the erotic art of seduction from their sisters, aunts, and other women of the tribe at about the age of twelve.

"And, Diego, rich as ever, my friend?" Bill questioned as he drank the fruity, sweet dark red wine from the cool silver cup.

"*Arvalie,* yes! I'm as rich as ever, but a poor man in the end because I give to my people. But today I'm richer still by your presence in my camp, my friend."

"Then accept this small gift as a token of our friendship," Bill said, handing Diego a heavy bag filled with gold doubloons. "Catlina, where is she?" questioned Bill.

"My daughter is with that Spanish *beng* [devil] in his castle. She thinks she has found where the plans to the fortifications that you seek are kept, but I fear that this Juan Martinez may suspect her. She has asked too many questions and shows too much interest in military matters for a common Gypsy girl. He is a *sarp*, a snake."

"How is she held?" Bill asked.

"She is not held against her will. She is there because he wants her. She is there because of you, my friend, and the information you wanted her to find. She risks all because of you. I can bring her back away from him at anytime. But she asks for you and would not leave until you came."

"Did she tell you where the plans were kept? Are they at El Morro?"

"No, they are not at the castle. The admiral keeps them at his residence in the city next to the plaza," said Diego. "It is impossible for Catlina alone to steal the heavy books. The volumes are too massive and too complicated to copy. The plans to the fortifications are kept in a closed room with no windows, behind a heavy iron door that is always locked. Only the Governor General and the Admiral have keys."

"How do you contact her?" asked Bill. "Does she ever come back to your camp?"

"The admiral always has her escorted by his soldiers. She can come and go as she wants, but never alone. Even when she comes here, it's with an escort of five soldiers. The window to her room at the admiral's residence opens onto Cable Obispo Street. Across this street is another residence, which she can see from her window. If I need to contact her, I leave a chalk mark on the wall of the building across the street from her window. She knows to look there for messages," Diego explained.

"I am here, my friend, and we must bring Catlina back, out of harm's way, and your tribe must once again move to the next port," replied Bill. "Do you know of Varadero, where the old abandoned salt mines are, just down the coast?"

"Yes, and there are salt caves there," said Diego.

"That's right. Begin moving your people and your wagons to Varadero. I have already arranged for one of my ships to meet us there. Hide in the caves away from the Spanish until my ship comes. Then load your wagons and people aboard the ship. But first I must meet with Catlina. Can you get word to her?"

"Yes, I will send Amaya into Havana to make the mark on the wall. As soon as she sees the sign, she will make an excuse to visit us."

"Lend me some clothes, and I will go with Amaya into Havana. I would like to see what I'm up against," Bill said.

After Bill dressed in a loose-fitting brown cotton peasant shirt and brown cotton pants with a drawstring at the waist and old brown sandals on his feet, he covered himself completely with a black course-wool hooded cloak that was similar to the *burnous* garment that he had seen the Berbers wear in North Africa. With an old leather bag hanging across his shoulder, he climbed onto the mule-drawn cart that Amaya had waiting, and they rode toward La Havana.

Havana was called the key to the New World because it was both the principal merchant port and naval base of the Spanish Americas and existed solely for the good of the mother country. The city was first located on the southern coast of Cuba but was relocated in 1519 to its present location. It had always been a ripe target for privateers to plunder, loot, and burn until Juan Bautista Antonelli, the Italian military engineer who had built the many other forts in the Spanish Caribbean, completed the construction of Castillo de los Tres Reyes del Morro—El Morro Castle—in 1630. Now the port and the city stood invincible, and all trade either coming from or going back to Spain came into Havana.

As Bill and Amaya approached the city, they stopped, and Bill covered his head and body and the leather satchel with the *burnous* and, leaving his companion, stepped down from the cart and walked down the fertile green hills and then through the cultivated tobacco fields that led toward the city of Havana. To the northeast across the bay sat the fortifications and lighthouse of El Morro; on the west side of the bay sat the city.

Bill walked to the city on the west side of the bay and headed for the Plaza de Armas. The idea of a *plaza* was a common feature to most Spanish settlements in the New World and was usually the military, administrative, and cultural center of the city or port. Covered in the dark cloak with head and shoulders bent like an old man, Bill's sandaled feet shuffled their way down Cable Obispo Street, which ran alongside the plaza. He passed Castillo de Real Fuerza, the Governor General's residence, and stood before a two-story building facing the street and glanced at the heavy wooden gate, guarded by two soldiers. He looked up at the high walls that enclosed the courtyard and the wide balcony windows that were open on the second floor. He ambled up and down the cobblestone boulevards of the city and through the narrow passageways that separated the buildings around the Admiral's home. After a careful survey of the area he found a place across from the massive wooden gate and slowly sat down, his back sliding against the wall of the building. Resting against the wall he pulled the dark hood of the *burnous* over his head, covering his unshaven face.

As evening approached and as bystanders filled the street, Bill cautiously moved to the building across from the admiral's residence, and using the chalk that Diego had given him, he drew a Byzantine cross with a crescent moon at the top-left corner. He hoped that Catlina would see this symbol from her window and recognize it as the sign that she must meet with him in her father's camp.

He sat across the street from the massive wooden gate for the rest of that day and into the night. He watched as the gate was opened then closed, and people came and went. On several occasions, Bill left his place against the wall and wandered along the streets around the admiral's home. As darkness fell, he climbed up a trellis to the flat roof of a building close-by, and hiding behind the low parapet, he removed his spyglass from the leather satchel and silently looked into the Admiral's closed courtyard, where more people came and went.

The next morning back on the street, he slouched against the wall opposite the gate and watched silently as Amaya's cart stopped in front of the building, and he saw Catlina, in a long low-cut red dress, climb onto the cart. Five Spanish cavalrymen thundered out of the compound, determined to escort Catlina wherever she might be going.

Bill's old nemesis, Don Juan Martinez de Palategui y Guzman Rocaberti, was the admiral of the fleet that protected the Spanish West Indies. With the threat of their treasure ports being invaded, Spain built massive fortifications in the New World. Admiral de Palategui was now the unquestioned naval commander responsible for these fortifications as well as the warships that both protected the convoys of treasure ships and the ports and, as such, held in his possession all the construction plans and descriptions of armaments for these locations. The blueprints for places like Puerto del Principe, Maracaibo, Vera Cruz, Portobelo, and Panama were all in the hands of a single individual. This codex of information was what Catlina had been looking for, what she risked her life for, and what Bill intended to steal.

Bill shuffled slowly out of the city, into the hills, and walked toward the Gypsy camp. The cart carrying Catlina was moving just about as fast as Bill could walk, and within a short time, he caught up with the caravan. The Spanish cavalry was doggedly still in attendance. Amaya and Catlina entered the camp while Bill, following a short distance behind, merged into the confusion of the Gypsies dismantling their lodgings. Catlina was met by her mother's embrace, and with her father, she entered one of the wagons. The Spanish horsemen dismounted and stood outside the back of the wagon. Bill discreetly entered the wagon from the front.

"Catlina," he said as he embraced her. He held her face in his hands and kissed her lips.

Her mother and father smiled, sitting by her side.

"My love, let us speak quickly about what I have discovered," she said as she pulled away from Bill's embrace. "The plans that you seek are not at the castle but in his residence." She quieted her excited voice as she realized that the guards were just outside the wagon. "He has spoken of an iron door, and I have seen him studying the documents in his library, but I don't know or have I ever seen the exact place where the vault is located." Her voice was now almost a whisper. "In two days there will be a banquette held at the castle. Everyone will be there, the house will be empty, and all the guards will be in attendance at the banquette. During the banquette is the time you can steal what you have been wanting." "Then you cannot return, Catlina. You must stay here and escape with your family," Bill pleaded.

"No, I must return, or he will be suspicious. Everything must appear as normal for you to succeed. I want to return. I want to kill him." Her dark eyes lit brighter than Bill had ever seen them, and for the first time he saw a side of Catlina that he had never seen before, a dark side that frightened him. "But you and I will have tonight, my love," she whispered into his ear.

Catlina left the wagon and walked toward the soldiers that had accompanied her to the village, who stood in a group beside their horses, flirting with Francisca, Natasha, and some of the other young Gypsy girls in the camp. Catlina pulled aside a tall sergeant from the group. "I'll be staying here with my family tonight, Sergeant," she informed him. "Not knowing our customs, you cannot realize that tonight will be a celebration of the baptism of one of the girls in our tribe. It is both a solemn and joyful event that I must attend because the girl is my goddaughter. You and your men will be my guests if you wish, or you can return to Havana if you like." She left the sergeant speechless and walked back toward the wagon.

While the main part of the camp was being shut down and loaded onto the wagons, in a small clearing some distance away from the settlement, Diego had spontaneously assembled long tables under a hastily erected tent where plates, cups, and clusters of bottles containing wine, beer, brandy, rum, and *rakia* began to appear. Cooking fires seemed to spring out of nowhere, and slabs of raw gray meat eventually rested across the coals on metal spits.

At dusk the music started: violins, guitars, singers, and drums. As if attracted to the music like moths to a candle flame, young girls began to dance, kicking dust up from under their booted feet into the dry air. Natasha, Francisca, and Dasha, Cat's cousin, whisked the Spanish soldiers under the tent and seated them at the table, pouring large silver chalices of *rakia* for each man. The two trained black bears hesitantly moved upright on their back legs, forearms pawing at the night to the music, and came into the clearing by the tent, led only by a young dark Gypsy girl of about twelve years old.

As the soldiers drank and ate, one brightly painted wagon pulled by two horses silently rolled out of the Gypsy camp into the black night toward a green meadow just outside the trees that sheltered the Gypsy's site. The brass bells that normally mark the progress of any Gypsy wagon had been removed; silenced in the darkness, the horses pulled the wagon farther and farther away from the campsite, and the Spanish soldiers—who were now being entertained with drink, music, dancing bears, and the vivacious Natasha, Francisca, and other young girls of the camp—never saw Catlina leave in the wagon.

Dasha held the four leather reins attached to the horses' snaffle bit between the fingers of her slim hands, just as her father had taught her. Each finger sensed the need of applying just the right amount of pressure on the bars across the horse's nose, tongue, and the corners of the mouth, where they would respond appropriately, never hurting but gently guiding. After venturing about a mile away from the camp, Dasha pulled the wagon to a stop under a tree and opened the small brightly colored wooden door that led from the carriage seat into the back of the wagon. Dasha saw Catlina perched on top of Bill on the brightly colored pillows at the back of the wagon. Cat's long brown bare legs were wrapped around Bill's body, her knees and thighs peeking from under her long skirt as she lustfully rode him; her large heavy breasts hung suspended from the front of her open blouse. Dasha undressed and moved next to Cat and Bill.

Dasha and Cat were cousins. Both had chosen the way of the *looverni* within their tribe. Catlina, being older, had trained Dasha for this profession, and they had seduced other men together on several occasions. It was something both enjoyed. As Dasha cradled her naked body into Bill's arms, Cat removed her clothing, and together, both Cat and Dasha knew exactly what to do for Bill's pleasure.

Raid on La Habana

October 1663, 7:00 p.m.
Cable Obispo Street, Havana, Cuba

On the night of the planned celebration at the castle, Bill once again sat across the street from the admiral's compound in his peasant clothing and the *burnous* pulled loosely around his body and head. A carriage approached. Catlina and the admiral stepped into the carriage. After the two passengers were comfortably seated, two black horses pulled the carriage onto Cable Obispo Street, and with the hollow echoes of the horse's hooves clopping against the cobblestone road, they disappeared into the night accompanied by eight ornately uniformed military horsemen. He sat and listened and watched from under his black cloak against the wall, a beggar, a vagabond, unnoticed by all but seeing everything.

After the carriage and soldiers disappeared down the street, Bill went silently over the wall, not through the wooden gate where the guards stood, into the admiral's home. The open verandas that he had seen from the rooftops greeted him as he climbed down the green leafy grape arbor that cast dimples of moonlight and shadows across the red brick courtyard enclosed by open balconies. A cistern that collected rainwater from the terra-cotta tiled roofs stood in the center of the courtyard, the dark water reflecting the lights from the lower floors of the building.

The young Aztec servant girl watched from the shadows as Bill dropped from the grape arbor that reached over the wall, into the courtyard, and entered the wide double doors that opened into the interior. She hid in the shadows and followed him silently as he searched the room.

Tall dark wooden cabinets, lavishly inlaid with ivory, and shell, stood against one white plastered wall. Soft orange-colored light from brass oil lamps hanging from the walls lit the room in translucent warmth. The cabinets were filled with leather-bound books; the raised hubbed spine of each book was deeply embossed with gold lettering identifying each volume. A sea chest that opened into an escritoire made of teak, bronze, and copper and inlaid with ivory Arabic script stood in the middle of the room. Other cabinets around the room were filled with colorful Inca, Aztec, and Mayan ceramics. A dazzling buon fresco map splashed across one entire wall, the rich vibrant pigments colorfully detailing every aspect of the Caribbean. Across the room from the fresco was a massive stone fireplace that jutted seven feet or more from the wall into the room. The wide open hearth seemed to spill onto the tiled floor of the room without a break, and the stone sides leading to the plaster wall were covered with intricately designed Persian rugs.

In his open sandals and hooded cape, Bill walked through the downstairs part of the house looking for the iron door that Catlina had described. He climbed the unguarded wide tiled stairway leading to the second floor. The second floor of the mansion left nothing to be desired. The walls of the hallway were covered with tapestries; the hardwood teak floors were covered with woven silk rugs. Silently, he searched the rooms, the corridors, the stairways; he pulled aside colorful tapestries hanging on the walls, looking for concealed openings. Upstairs and downstairs he searched but could find nothing.

In desperation Bill returned to the admiral's study. He had missed something, but what? Sitting at the desk, Bill's mind wandered as he watched the dancing shadows of the oil lamps playing upon the walls. He was thinking how unusual the construction of the fireplace was. Why did it extend into the room so far when it very easily could have been built back into the wall? And why did the hearth seem to spill out into the room? Of course! Bill ran to the side of the fireplace and pulled first one then the next Persian rug aside. Nothing!

In the darkness, a small brown-skinned woman in sandals came to his side.

"The door?" she whispered. "Are you looking for the door?"

"Yes," Bill quietly answered a hush started voice as he saw the girl for the first time.

"You a pirate?" she asked inquisitively.

"No, my dear. I'm an English officer."

"I am Tz'iken. I'll show you where the door is if you'll take me with you."

"Of course, you can come with me," Bill replied.

Moving to the side of the fireplace, Tz'iken said, "Here, the door is here." And she pushed her hand across the stone that slid the massive wall apart, revealing an iron door.

Bill quietly tested the massive iron door, and he found that it was bolted. Three blue-black tempered steel hinges held the four-inch-thick iron door inside the stone casing at the right, and on the left side a polished bronze extrusion plate of a Dutch elbow lock was unmovable in his hands.

"I don't have the key," said the girl. "The admiral always carries it with him."

With the small brown girl standing next to him, Bill removed the green claylike substance with the familiar smell of almonds that the Persian had given him from his leather bag and packed the moldable, soft puttylike material around the steel hinges and down the right side of the door. He inserted a small brass tube containing a glass flute of sulfuric acid and a spring-loaded striker that was held in place under tension by a thin copper wire. He crushed the thin brass walls of the tube to break the glass, and the acid slowly began to eat through the copper wire holding back the striker, giving him time to run outside of the building, into the courtyard, and to the massive wooden gate that led onto the street.

While the acid was still eating through the first thin copper wire inside the brass tube, Bill and the girl placed another mound of wax and another brass tube on the gate. He crushed the glass capsule inside the second tube now fixed to the gate and ran back toward the building. A moment later, the acid dissolved the copper wire in the first tube on the iron door, and the striker plunged down into the hollow center of the container, hitting a mixture of sulfur, sugar, and potassium perchlorinate, which created a small blast that detonated the soft almond-smelling explosive wax into a much larger explosion.

The Persian had explained to Bill, "This claylike material and the brass device is simply knowledge of the elements. The Persians were the foremost chemists of the Mediterranean when Europeans were having difficulty making clay pots. The caliphate of Cordoba built a vast library that rivaled the one that was destroyed at Alexandria. Much of the knowledge contained in that vast library has never been shared with you infidels."

Then the Persian hinted with a smile, "Or maybe it's your English sorcery, magic, or alchemy, or maybe the will of Allah. The explosive clay is mostly a mixture of distilled potassium salts made from leaching potash, and then the dried crystals are ground into a fine white powder, which is distilled again, mixed with another chemical, and then molded into the wax along with a reddish-brown flammable liquid that the Persians called naphtha, the Greeks called it median oil, that I found in the mangrove swamp where we obtain our bitumen for waterproofing the roofs of the buildings on the island. A very similar mixture was used by the Greeks to make 'Greek Fire'—bitumen or pitch, sulfur, saltpeter, and tree resin. The clay can't be detonated with a black powder fuse. You have to use the brass tube to create a small explosion that will ignite the clay to create the much larger explosion. The clay produces an explosion many times greater than black powder. So be very careful how much you use."

As the smoke cleared, Bill held the fragile young woman close. He considered the fact that he probably had used too much of the explosive wax. Not only was the heavy iron door torn from its hinges, but most of the stone fireplace and much of the admiral's study had also been destroyed. As Bill ran into the shattered, smoke-filled room, pushing aside the bookshelves and desk that now cluttered the floor, blocking his way to the vault, the second explosion at the gate shook the whole building and killed both guards standing outside the gate. Bill picked up one of the oil lamps that still smoldered and gently brought life back to the flame, providing him light as he moved across the stone rubble of the fireplace that had once formed the vault.

At the back of the room he found what he was looking for—several dozen large, heavy, thick, leather-covered volumes of drawings, written construction notes, and diaries. Hefting just one of the books into his arms, Bill realized that each of these massive tomes must weigh thirty pounds or more. Looking at the girl by his side, he noticed that black soot covered her face. "We must be a sight," Bill said, smiling.

"I trust I find you well, my friend?" came a familiar voice through the blackness and smoke.

"Diego?" Bill questioned.

Diego and several other Gypsies moved rapidly through the shambles carrying lanterns to light their way. They worked in silence, quickly picking up the heavy books inside the admiral's vault and loading each precious volume onto the mule cart that waited outside with Amaya.

"If you were going to steal something, my friend, you should have asked a Gypsy. I think your eyes were bigger than your hands. How did you ever imagine that you could take all these books alone?" stated Diego.

"I had Amaya. I was not alone," Bill feebly responded. "And I had this girl, Tz'iken." Bill pushed the girl in front of Diego. "Take her with you."

Diego, looking around the smoke-filled room, said, "Let's move quickly. My men have taken care of the few guards that were stationed around the town. There are horses waiting on the street, and we must leave."

Outside on Cable Obispo Street, crowds of people were starting to gather in hesitant wonder at what the explosion had been and why men were running from the admiral's home, but they were mostly peasants and not the military. The vast majority of the military, the soldiers and the guards stationed at Havana, were across the bay at Castillo el Morro where a grand banquette was being held. Juan Martinez and Cat were attending these festivities.

"Take the wagon with our treasure and Tz'iken out of the city. Get your people to Varadero and wait for my ship as we had planned. Captain Brossard commands the *Blanche Sorciere*. He has my instructions. He will meet you there," explained Bill. "Somehow I will find Cat."

Diego, the mule cart, and the Gypsy horsemen rode down Cable Obispo Street, through the plaza, and into the night. Captain Walker now melted back into the crowd that was gathering around the admiral's gate. His face and hands were still covered with the black soot from the explosion. The sound of the soldiers' horses could be heard in the distance as they came through the city, the steeds' metal shoes hitting the cobblestone streets as they ran. Bill blended into the crowd. As the men on horseback came to the shattered gate and the sight of smoking rubble inside the Admiral's compound, they began to shout curses into the crowd of peasants that stood in the street. From horseback the soldiers chased down unwary peasants, flogging them with their short whiplike leather riding crops and screamed questions into the crowd. "¿Quién hizo esto? [Where is the culprit?] ¿Qué pasó aquí? [What has happened here?]" the soldiers shouted.

"Fue los gitanos." Peasant after peasant replied in fear. "It was the Gypsies," they cried.

What Bill had feared and why he wanted to go alone had happened. If he could have managed to steal the volumes without Diego's direct involvement, then little blame might have fallen on either Catlina or her tribe. But now with Gypsy horsemen being seen and easily identified because no one but a Gypsy could hope to own a horse as fine as what the Gypsies have and no one can ride like a Gypsy, they all were doomed. Bill said a silent payer for the other Gypsy tribes on the island. While Diego's clan might escape, the other tribes would suffer the wrath of the Admiral's rage. So would Catlina as soon as the Admiral discovered that Gypsies were involved in stealing his fortification plans.

Eventually the ornate black carriage pulled by the two black horses and the accompanying horsemen that Bill had seen Catlina leave with earlier in the evening came to a rest in front of the shattered gate. Bill watched as the Admiral stepped out of the carriage and pushed past one of the soldiers that came running to his side from the smoking building. More soldiers gathered around the carriage. Other soldiers were running to and from the Admiral's residence. An officer, coming from inside the residence, approached the Admiral's coach, and Bill could see but not hear the three men speaking.

What fire there was had been extinguished, and now just smoke hung in the air like a low cloud. The distinctive smell of burnt hardwood and the pungent aroma of naphtha still lingered in the air as Catlina gracefully stepped down from the carriage, an officer at her hand, the Admiral still talking with the two officers on the other side of the carriage.

Bill watched her as her feet touched the ground. She fluffed the petticoats under her black low-cut dress, pulled her black hair back across her shoulders, and smiling at the young officer holding her hand, she discreetly glanced toward the wall where Bill had left the warning symbol. As her head tilted, Bill knew that she had seen him, but her face showed no sign that she was aware of any danger or his presence. In fact, it would appear that there was not a thought in her mind as she walked, her graceful steps almost like the dance she knew so well, smiling and laughing at the arm of the young officer beside her, to the other side of the coach and into the arms of the Admiral.

With the turmoil of discovery somewhat subsiding, tempers settled, crowds thinned, the smoke dissipated, the soldiers relaxed their weapons, the horses calmed, and Bill moved closer to where Catlina and the Admiral stood talking with the two officers. With his cloak pulled over his head, peasant clothing, and sandals, he was just part of the throng that lingered curiously on the street. All saw him, but no one noticed him as he slouched down inside the dark robe, as an old man would, his slow, scuffling sandaled feet dragging the ground with each step.

Bill approached the carriage. Just within earshot he heard, "And it seems, Excellency, that a dozen Gypsy horsemen were seen. A cart was also seen," stated one of the officers.

"Your residence is secure, Excellency," stated another officer, coming to the Admiral's side.

"What did they steal? What was the purpose of this attack?" the Admiral asked.

"The vault was broken into. The stone room, the iron door was shattered. I am informed, by an expert in these matters, that it would have taken four or five kegs of gunpowder to do this much damage. It's not imaginable, Your Excellency, that anyone could bring five kegs of gunpowder into the city and then find a way into your residence and then have the opportunity to place those kegs at the exact hidden point of your iron door. It's not possible, Your Excellency, but that seems to be what happened."

"You say Gypsies? Yes? But wait... Catlina, my darling. My captain tells me that this offense is..."

Bill could not hear all the words.

The admiral then struck Catlina a savage blow across her face! Bill jumped forward, almost as a reflex, but was pulled back from his rage by a combination of common sense, helplessness, and realizing that he could do nothing at this moment to help her.

"Juan!" she cried.

Bill could just hear some of her cries as the officers dragged her away.

"Tie her and take her to my chambers. Do nothing to her. It will be my pleasure to question her," Bill heard the Admiral command.

The once admiring officers and soldiers now thrust Catlina between them. Unable to move, she went limp in their strong arms, placid in only that moment but knowing the revenge in her heart. Catlina was not a Gypsy woman to trifle with. By the age of fifteen, she had already killed one man with a knife; he had raped one of the girls from her tribe under her care. By the time she was twenty, it was said that she had killed another man with a small thin knife in bed as he slept or, some say, as they made love. Her slight build, youth, and beauty had deceived many into believing that she was helpless.

Several hours later Martin entered the room where Catlina was tied across the bed. Her hands were attached to each bedpost at the top of the bed, and her ankles were tied to the bottom of the bed's wooden frame. She was lovely, bright, alive, yet with a lustful hidden danger that the admiral, unfortunately, didn't recognize.

"My soldiers are on their way to your camp, my dear. They have my orders to kill everyone." The Admiral walked casually around the bed where Catlina was tied. He drew his knife and slowly cut the clothing from her body until she lay naked. "What might you say for yourself?" he questioned.

Cat lay silently tied to the bed as Martin walked around the room.

"Have I ever told you about my training in the monastery? As a young man, I wore the black *cappa* of the Dominican Order of the Inquisition. I still wear the ring," he said as he showed her the silver ring with the crossed swords over a crucifix. "Your body has given me much pleasure over these last few months, and I'm sorry that must end. Your death, me love, will either be a cruel one with much suffering, which I can assure you I am an expert at, or a quick ending without torment if you speak. The choice is yours, my dear."

Juan paced the floor beside the bed where Catlina lay naked and bound, toying with his Castilian double-bladed dagger as he walked around her.

Brooding and despondent, Martin stood next to the bed. "This is not your doing, my dear. I know that. It could never have been your idea, and I know that it has nothing to do with your family. Only one man could have contrived a plot as bold as this. Only one man could have done this—Bloody Bill Walker."

Bill climbed the grape arbor on the side of the house to the balcony that wrapped around the second floor of the building, his dark cloak masking his presence from the soldiers in the courtyard and on the street. After climbing ships' rigging all his life, the wide, thick grapevines offered little difficulty as he darted up the face of the building to the open veranda.

"Juan, free my hands and I will tell you everything," Catlina pleaded. "If you care for me, come to me now, and I will tell you all I know. I am not a part of this thing, my love, believe me. My family has cast me out. I went to our village, and my father told me that I was expelled from the tribe, an outcast, because of my love for you. I only have you now. I'm not a part of my people." Catlina pleaded as she wriggled her nude body salaciously back and forth on the bed. "Cut me loose, and I'll tell you where they have gone."

The Admiral paced the floor and finally came to the head of the bed, where Catlina was tied. He took his dagger and cut the ropes binding her hands. As she sat up in bed, he moved to the foot of the bed and freed her feet. Sitting by the bedside, her long black hair fell across her breasts and face, and Juan could not see the eyes or imagine the sinister desire in this woman. Her long heavily lacquered fingernails were just as sharp and deadly as the admiral's Castilian dagger, and in the Gypsy camps, she had been trained how to use her nails like stilettos.

Bill, coming through the open second-story shuttered balcony door into the room, found Catlina's naked body straddled across the Admiral. Her hands clutched his thin neck and face. Her red lacquered fingernails drew blood from his gouged left eye that dripped down his white throat onto the crimson shirt he wore, where it pooled as a black stain. Martin struggled to bring the knife he held over his head, and the hand thrust down toward Catlina's bare back.

Bill quickly grabbed Martin's arm and pulled the dagger from his hand just before it would have plunged into Catlina. "My god, Catlina!" Bill said, laughing. "Don't kill my friend Martin. Leave the killing to me." He said this in a joking, offhanded manner. And he pulled the naked young muscular body of the long-haired Gypsy girl off the dazed Spaniard.

"Martin, my lad!" Bill exclaimed to the admiral as he dragged Catlina to his side. Holding a sword in his hand, Bill rested the blade between the man's legs. "Haven't you learned by now to never trust a woman? Especially a Gypsy woman."

"Ah, Walker. I thought I had killed you, but yet here you are," declared the Admiral as he held his hand across his face, wiping the blood coming from his eye. "You know, of course, that you and the girl will never leave Havana alive."

"Would you burn us alive as heretics in the name of your church and the Inquisition as you have other English sailors?"

"But of course. I would have no choice in the matter."

"Tie him," Bill told Catlina. "Tie him securely."

"No! Kill him," Catlina demanded in a stern voice.

"Not this time, my dear. Not today. No, we'll leave Martin here. After all, he now has a souvenir from his time with you: a missing eye. Maybe he can explain that to his King, and maybe he can explain how he has lost all the Spanish plans for their fortifications to a single English sailor and a Gypsy girl. I understand that the Spanish King is quite severe in punishing inept officers and officials."

"I'll see you dead first!" the admiral shouted as Catlina pushed a cloth gag into his mouth.

"We'll see," Bill said, smiling. "We'll see. *Adios*, Martin, my friend." Bill turned away from the admiral, clinging to Catlina. He threw his cloak over her naked shoulders and carried her to the window. He turned and, taking her arms around his neck, climbed from the window, down the grape arbor, and to the street.

"Is she dead?" Diego softly questioned as Bill climbed down the trellis with Catlina's body hanging from his back. "She is dead, my son?" he asked again.

"She is not dead, Diego," Bill whispered as he came off the arbor and onto the deserted street. "She is not dead, Diego," he said again.

"Is the *sarp* dead?"

"No, Diego, the Admiral is not dead."

"Is anyone dead?" Diego asked as he threw up his arms in frustration. "What kind of a Gypsy do you ever hope to be if you don't kill someone?" Diego exclaimed disgustedly in a muffled voice that evaporated into the night air as he pulled Cat onto his horse.

Come to Quarters

6 October 1663, 2:00 a.m.
Varadero Bay, Cuba

"She's in shock," Brossard announced, standing over the unconscious body of Tz'iken, who was lying on Brossard's bed in his cabin aboard the *White Witch*. "I've seen this sort of thing before. She's healthy enough. In a few days she'll come around."

Dasha knelt beside the girl, offering sips of rum and bathing her face with a moist cloth.

"Coriancha," the girl whispered. "Coriancha." She then fell into a restless sleep.

"Do we set sail, Captain?" Brossard asked, turning to Bill as he walked to the large table where Diego and Bill sat drinking rum from tankards.

"Take her out, Mr. Brossard," Bill commanded.

Brossard left the cabin, and Bill could hear Brossard's voice shouting orders to the crew and the sound of bare feet on the deck overhead.

Bill sat thinking for a moment and then said to Diego, "Very well. We must get back to the island without delay." He stood and walked out of the cabin. Cat and Dasha followed him as he climbed the steps to the quarterdeck, where Brossard stood shouting orders.

"Lieutenant, Spanish warships are in the harbor. Once Martin frees himself, he'll send soldiers into the hills to find the Gypsies. He'll also undoubtedly send his warships now in the harbor to stop all outgoing vessels. I think that we might need to escape. No lights and no noise."

Brossard laughed. "Aye aye, Captain," Brossard said and moved forward, now with a purpose.

It was a dark night; there was no moon, and even the stars appeared only dimly in the sky. Bill held Cat by his side as the sandglass was turned, but the bell marking the beginning of the midwatch never rang, and all the lights above deck had been extinguished. In the black night, the mainsail lifted with wind and pushed the hull of the wooden-framed vessel overloaded with Gypsy wagons, dancing girls, horses, and two bears into the deep waters that ran just a few feet below her gunnels.

Carried by the gentle breezes that blew from the gulf of the Americas across that wide body of water and the currents that lapped onto Cuba, the ship slowly pushed into the darkness. As the ship moved blindly ahead, young Dasha came to the other side of Bill and clung to his arm.

"On deck," came a soft voice from a seaman stationed at the mast high above the deck.

"Two points off the starboard bow, ship's lights, monsieur," the lookout whispered to the captain below.

"Come to quarters," Bill said to the first mate. "To be on the safe side, man your guns and have the gun crew stand by. But don't light your matches. Send marksmen aloft and assemble more on deck. Get the women below."

"Oui, Capitaine," said the mate. "Quarters it is."

As the overloaded ship chopped silently through the black night, Bill sat in the cabin below the quarterdeck with Brossard. "I must return to England," he said quietly to the Frenchman. "I received a letter from my father, and there is a matter of family business that requires my presence at home," he announced offhandedly. "On my father's instructions, I will not sail the *Commencement* back to England. Doing so would both limit our future gains here and unduly announce my absence from these waters and my arrival in England. With your assistance, I hope to maintain the belief that I remain here and am still in command of the *Commencement* during the few months that I will be gone. I have decided therefore to leave you, Mr. Brossard, in command. But you must heed the words of both Mr. Cribb and Big Daniel in my absence. They are both sound, good-thinking mates, and you would do well to take any advice that either might offer. Upon your life, Mr. Brossard, my absence must not be known. After unloading our Gypsy friends at the island, we will take the *Witch* and rendezvous at sea with one of my father's West Indiaman on her return voyage to England."

Lloyd's Coffeehouse

12 February 1664, 10:00 a.m.
London, England

Sitting at a small table in Lloyd's Coffeehouse on Tower Street, Bill watched in amazement as one messenger after another came running into the building and then left just as rapidly after handing over some slip of paper or carefully whispering a secret to the man behind the tall counter. In the background, men in black suits and white shirts, suspended on tall ladders, crawled like spiders across high dusty blackboard walls, posting updated information in sharp white chalk notations.

"This establishment," his father said, "is a gathering place for investors, merchants, and shipowners. They come here, my boy, to listen to the news concerning ship arrivals and departures and prices offered for the cargos. See the blackboard against that wall? It lists every English ship that is afloat today in every part of the world. The name of the ship's master, the destination, the cargo, the port it sailed from, and the date is marked alongside. That board over there shows the at-port prices for a cargo. Our spies keep us well-informed about merchant ships of other countries. So we usually know who is shipping what and to where.

"William, what you see around you is now the real power behind the new British Empire. Trade, son, is what makes us great. Not your Royal Navy warships that you are so fond of. The navy only exists to assure that trade continues. We are no longer an agrarian society, no longer lord and serf, landowner and peasant. We now have an emerging middle class of merchants. This new merchant class has created the wealth that now drives our country. These merchants build vast country homes and estates outside the cities. These merchants are the investors in the Royal Africa Company, the East India Company, and the West Indies Association. These investors are sitting in this room, and they also sit in Parliament. Look around you, son. The people you see here are the British economy, the New British Empire.

"For the last century, the slave trade has grown into the primary constituent of our financial system. The investors at Lloyd's make their money from slavery in some form, either directly or indirectly. And the economic base of most of the African states like Oyo, Dahomey, Benin, Asante, and, of course, Zanzibar are all funded off the slave trade. You may not realize this, but Britain is now only second to the Portuguese in the volume of slaves sold. It's what drives it all.

"But with the higher profits, the risks have also increased. Do you realize that if a single merchant shipowner were to lose one ship's cargo, it could mean financial ruin, bankruptcy? That's why many of us here at Lloyd's are starting to come together as, shall we say, members or subscribers to both pool our resources and spread our risk associated with the maritime trade and shipping across a broader base. One of these members is Sir Harold Dobbs. You know Sir Harold, of course. He is your mother's nephew. I would like you to meet with him tonight and hear a proposition he has for you."

"Certainly, Father. Would that be at the Club?" asked Bill.

"Oh, I think so, say around nine. The Club is exclusively loyalist nowadays and of the aristocrat fashion, after a sort, so wear your uniform," his father said.

Sir Harold Dobbs

12 February 1664, 6:30 p.m.
London, England

William, arriving at the building on James Street that evening wearing his Royal Navy uniform but without his powdered white wig, was stopped at the door.

"Whom is your party, sir?" asked the doorman, a big, bulky bruiser who was dressed in black-and-white formal attire. Apparently a very pleasant individual, but his size alone would have overwhelmed any timid man. His left hand presented a silver salver, and Bill placed his engraved calling card on the brightly polished silver tray.

"Sir Harold is expecting me. Please say Lieutenant Walker," replied Bill.

The idea of a gentlemen's club seems to be, much like Lloyd's, another innovation and experiment in English culture generated by the new wealthy merchants of Britain. As a members-only private establishment, these few new enterprises were finding their place in the West End of London. To the north of James Street was Piccadilly, to the west was Green Park, and to the south was James's Park. Haymarket Street was one block over. And the Haymarket Theatre and Her Majesty's Theatre, also located on Haymarket Street, were filled most nights with an audience of young middle-class gentleman and ladies anxious to see the next Shakespeare play. Haymarket Street, aside from its theatres and culture, was also reputed to be the London center of high-fashion prostitution, where adventurous, free-spirited, bold women might seek out the company of an eligible man for the evening—of course, with a price.

While the English aristocracy had no need of exclusive social meeting places and the British military had always had their own exclusive clubs, the gentlemen merchants were now creating fellowships characterized by their members' trade, political identity, or interest in sports, travel, literature, or some other pursuit. The first clubs in the Liberty of Westminster were built by the same architects who were constructing the townhouses in the same area of London and the country houses outside the cities and had the same types of interiors. These clubs for many became, in effect, a second home. Members might live at their club during the time that they were conducting business in London and then travel back to their country estates when not engaged. Most clubs, while exclusive, contained a few rooms in which members could dine and entertain nonmembers.

Bill unbuckled his saber and placed the French .40 caliber flintlock pistol into the hands of another attendant. The streets of London were controlled by gangs of thieves, murderers, and crooks. Any unarmed, unsuspecting individual walking London's streets was in danger. Bill removed most of his weapons. He still had the ten-inch double-edge thrusting dagger cradled reassuringly at the center of his spine. Standing in the spacious well-appointed foyer just inside the entrance, he waited until the doorman returned.

"This way, Lieutenant Walker. Sir Harold and his guest are expecting you."

Bill was escorted through several rooms that apparently served various functions into a dining room. As they walked to the dining room, the man said, "My name is Willis, sir. If I can be of any further assistance to you while you are a guest with us, don't hesitate to have one of the stewards send for me." Willis led Bill to a table in the ornate dining room where Harold Dobbs and Bill's father were sitting.

Entertainments such as musical performances, singers, or plays were not a feature of this sort of club. These were quiet places in the center of London where gentlemen could relax with friends, have an excellent meal, a good wine, an exceptional brandy, and maybe play a game of cards.

"Lieutenant Walker of His Majesty's Royal Navy," Willis announced to the guests seated at the table.

"Bill, my boy," his father said as he pulled away from the table. Standing, he shook Bill's hand. "You remember Sir Harold, I'm sure."

Sir Harold also stood and greeted Bill with a warm handshake as well. Bill was offered a chair, and the three men settled at the table.

"William, a glass of wine? Your father and I have just opened this marvelous French blend." Sir Harold poured Bill a glass of red cabernet into the waiting crystal glass goblet that sat before his place at the table.

As Bill settled at the table and drank his first taste of the magnificent wine, Sir Harold commented in an offhanded fashion, "Your voyage back to London was pleasant, I hope."

"Quite so," replied William.

"No difficulty leaving your duties in the Caribbean?"

"None whatsoever, Sir Harold," Bill replied. "I cherish every chance to return to England and visit my family."

"Bill, Sir Harold has an idea and a proposition that he would like to present to you," his father said. "I am, as you may well understand later, in favor with Sir Harold's plan, but your involvement in part or in whole is your decision."

"William, I understand that you have been in the West Indies for some time now?" asked Sir Harold.

"Since 1654, sir," Bill stated. "I had the honor to have served as a midshipman under Admiral William Penn when he took his fleet across the Atlantic to the West Indies to capture Spanish territory. As you may know, we had first attempted to take Hispaniola and set siege at Santo Domingo. That attempt failed. The next year we captured Jamaica and Port Royal. On the fleet's return to England, I was promoted to lieutenant and given command of a captured Dutch vessel, which was to stay at Port Royal for its protection. Governor Edward D'Oley arrived in '57. My ship was commissioned as a private man-of-war along with several others, mainly English captains and their vessels that came out of Tortuga. Governor D'Oley then issued instructions and letters of marque. We were to protect Jamaica from the Spanish and retaliate against any Spanish intrusion."

"Very well, so you know these waters and the other captains under letters?" asked Sir Harold.

"Yes, sir, I know the waters well. And I know the captains and their ships."

"Maybe, if you don't mind my lecturing, we might begin with a little history," Sir Harold stated. "As you may know, the English were not the first to settle in the Caribbean. After some negotiations with the Spanish and a very restrictive treaty that only benefited the dons, St. Lucia Island in the early sixteen hundreds was our first attempt, but the native Carib Indians drove us out. Oliver Leigh then landed on an uninhabited island he called Barbados, which he, of course, claimed for England. Barbados was our only colony in the West Indies for many years until Penn captured Jamaica from the Spanish. The Spanish and their ally, the Portuguese, of course, control everything in the New World. French raiding ships plague Spanish shipping, and the French hold small isolated island strongholds. But the Spanish hardly bother with these. The Dutch are just now venturing into the Caribbean. While the French might have hopes of colonization, the Dutch are by nature merchants—freebooters. They hope to break the dependence of the Spanish colonies' trade that is now restricted to the mother country.

"To finance this expansion into the New World, the Dutch formed the Dutch West Indies Company in 1621. Around that same time the British House of Commons chartered the British West Indies Association. King James I granted the Earl of Carlise, under this West Indies Association, proprietary rights to the English Caribees, which was roughly defined as anything between ten and twenty degrees north latitude. The Dutch, French, Spanish, Portuguese, and now the English are all competing for colonies in the Caribbean. And why do you think that every nation wants colonies in the Southern Americas and the Caribbean?"

"I don't know, sir," replied Bill. "Gold?"

"Sugar, my boy! Sugar can't be grown but in a few places on earth. Why, do you realize that sugar does not grow, cannot be grown, anywhere in Europe? Can't be done, wrong climate, you see. And to grow sugar, you need slaves. Right now all the sugar in the world comes from the Caribbean, and the price for sugar continues to increase every day. And as the price of sugar goes up, the price for slaves increases as more and more sugar plantations are developed. Sugar, slaves, and munitions! It's a cash crop with every voyage. We double our investment by selling munitions made in England to the African warlords, who then sell us slaves that we ship to the Americas. Those slaves then sold on the auction blocks double our investment once again. The sugar that our ships bring back to England is sold at ten times the price that it cost us to manufacture the munitions that we make in England. We sell modern weapons for slaves and then sell the slaves for sugar. My god, for every shilling invested, we make fifty back in profit."

A steward approached the table where Bill and the other men were sitting. "May I bring another bottle of wine, gentlemen, or would you prefer to dine? Tonight we have an exceptional standing rib roast with cabernet au jus, carrots, onions, parsnips, and turnips served with a light, creamy horseradish sauce."

"Yes, Williams, I think that the rib roast will suit our company tonight. Thank you for your suggestion," Sir Harold dictated as the senior club member and therefore the appropriate one at the table who should make the decision as to the meal.

A frown crossed Bill's face. *Turnips. I hate turnips*, he thought to himself. But the Club was not a tavern or boardinghouse were vittles were ordered a la carte. No, tables were served much like you would find if you were to by chance visit in someone's country home outside the city.

As the steward left the table, Sir Harold continued. "The Spanish and of course the Portuguese for the last century continue to extend their domination both over the islands of the Indies and over the mainland of the Americas and the South Seas. Spain is now systematically ransacking the New World for treasures of all kinds and shipping the spoils back to Europe. These riches finance Spain's conquest in Europe, and a large portion of these spoils find their way to the Vatican and the pope, who unquestionably supports and encourages Spain's interest. Portuguese interest now falls under Spanish control. While the gold, silver, and jewels coming out of the New World are quite profitable, no doubt, the sugar, cattle, and timber that their colonies export are the real treasures. And in the end, those colonies will be of more value than all the gold and silver that the Spanish can take out of the New World. All Spanish and Portuguese trade is, however, restricted. Everything from the New World has to, by royal decree, go back to Spain.

"Just this last week, the Venetian ambassador here in London reported that the Spanish in the West Indies had recently captured two English merchant vessels. These Spanish brigands reportedly cut off the hands, feet, noses, and ears of the crews and smeared them with honey. Then they tied the mutilated captives to trees, where they were tortured by flies and other insects. When His Majesty's Court questioned these acts, the Spanish pled that these prisoners were freebooters, scallywags, pirates, not merchants. But Pope Alexander's bull divided the New World between Spain and Portugal, therefore making all foreign trespassers in the Indies pirates. Spain and Portugal's insistence that her colonist should only trade with the home country makes the most innocent of English merchants a smuggler or worse," Sir Harold stated.

"I'm aware of the Spanish atrocities in the Indies, sir," Bill stated. "I witness them daily."

Williams, the steward, and five waiters under his direction served the meal from a wheeled cart brought to the table. Individual plates were served by the attendants. Then dishes and bowls were left on the table, which could accommodate further appetites. Two more bottles of wine were brought to the table and opened.

"Thank you, Williams," Sir Harold announced in compliment to the steward. After Williams assured that everything was in order, he and the attendants left the table.

As they ate, Sir Harold continued. "Thomas Modyford, do you know of him, William?" asked Sir Harold. Before Bill could comment, Sir Harold continued. "Modyford is the son of the mayor of Exeter. He has family connections to the Duke of Albemarle. In '47, he immigrated to Barbados as a young man with other family members in the opening stages of the English Civil War. He had £1,000 for a down payment on a plantation and £6,000 to commit in the next three years. Modyford soon was dominant in Barbados island politics as the Cromwell government came to power. He was able to appear to support the Roundheads and the Loyalists, by the way. He eventually rose to be Speaker of the House of Assembly just before Charles was returned to power and now sits, temporarily of course, as Governor of Barbados. But his loyalty is somewhat in question, placing him in an awkward situation with the restoration of the English monarchy due to his past support of Cromwell."

"As you know, Jamaica is now the most important stronghold of British power in the Caribbean. Thomas Modyford and his brother James are attempting—no, let me state that differently. They are bribing the members of the Commissioners of the Commonwealth for the position of Governor of Jamaica to be granted to James. They both have used their influence to discredit Lord Windsor's leadership as Governor in Jamaica and claim that he alone refuses to stop the privateers from attacking Spanish ships—which all sounds good in Court and provides Charles with a scapegoat. So a show must be made of poor Lord Windsor. But as I have stated, Thomas is not currently in favor with the King, and poor Thomas must be dealt with, but not in a fashion where he loses dignity, at least publically. And of course, we can't allow the Modyfords' control as governor of both Jamaica and Barbados. Any questions thus far, gentlemen?" asked Sir Harold.

He continued without pause, "Colonel James Modyford is assuming that he will receive the position of governor and is also asking for a royal license to ship convicted felons from England and Ireland to Jamaica. If that happens, it would change Jamaica from a trading port to a plantation-based economy. By the way, both Thomas and James have large holdings in the West Indies Association. Jamaica is our only fortified foothold in the West Indies, and all things considered, a scolded Thomas Modyford, removed as governor of Barbados, might be exactly the kind of new governor that we need to replace Lord Windsor."

As the meal ended, Sir Harold asked, "Another glass of this excellent wine? Or would you prefer brandy? And we can move to the open study by the fire."

A small, quiet open study was the second room where members could entertain nonmember guests. The room's walls were covered with mahogany bookshelves, colorfully woven tapestries, and gilded framed paintings depicting warships and naval heroes in full dress uniforms. The floor was polished teak planking, and the ceiling was covered with rolled, embossed copper metallic tiles. Gaslights on the walls covered the room with a soft glow that spread across the massive volumes of leather-bound books on the library shelves and dimly lit the paintings and tapestries, slurries of black soot spiraled onto the copper ceilings overhead. Heavy brown leather club chairs were gathered around the fireplace. Being a nonmember room, there were no other guests seated around the fireplace. In fact, there were no other guests in the quiet, isolated room.

Williams brought a tray with three bulb-shaped crystal brandy glasses and a quart of caramel-colored cognac in a crystal decanter. He poured a minute quantity of the brandy into a large concave silver spoon, added a pinch of gunpowder that settled to the bottom of the silver bowl, and then he ignited the mixture. If the gunpowder took fire in a flash when the spirits were consumed by the flame, then the liquor was good.

The French controlled the wine, brandy, and spirits imports throughout Europe. Rum was made in the New World, and England produced little more than gin.

The flash in the silver spoonlike dish consumed everything. The simple test certified that this bottle was good brandy, and Williams poured the caramel liquid into each man's glass.

"My boy, England is struggling for her very existence. Cromwell bankrupted the country, you know. Now we're fighting a kind of war where the economic life of England rests in the hands of a few people. We are losing vast amounts of commerce and our opportunity in the West Indies because of Spain's dominance. With the wealth that funnels into Spain from the New World, no European country can stand against them. The French and the Dutch are also taking their toll, further limiting our trade. The cost of maintaining a fleet to defend our interest in the colonies is beyond what England can afford. Most of our limited resources are now going into India. But even there, it's not the Royal Navy that backs our colonies. It's private interest embedded in the East India Company. Their private warships and private colonial armies, all under the Crown, mind you, but paid for by the East India Company. Charles and the Crown have just been tentatively restored, but now neither side in England's government wishes to empower either a king or chancellery or prime minister with the power of a navy or army capable of any force. The Crown can't legally commit to at this point in time to the defense of her colonies. We must therefore depend on, very unofficially, of course, private vessels that appear to be acting on their own. And while at least in the Caribe individual privateers like yourself and others have offered some relief, they are, for the most part, just blockade runners. With each country demanding that their colonies sell and buy only from the mother country, you scoundrels, no offense, in the Caribe for most of the year only pick up and carry contraband goods from port to port, defying the various European nations' blockades. You of course make a tidy profit along the way. But you only attack Spanish treasure ships if the opportunity presents, the weather is good, and the odds are unquestionably in your favor. There is not a fighting force under a unified command with a single purpose. Unfortunately, most are rogues who fight mainly for profit, if it suites them. They trade contraband goods and win prize, not battles. And more importantly, their primary goal is to snatch some unsuspected Spanish treasure, not in destabilizing the Spanish and Dutch colonies and the sugar plantations," Sir Harold stated.

The three men sat by the fire in the warm leather club chairs and continued their discussion, brandy snifters in hand, warming by the fire.

"William," his father softly said, "Sir Harold believes that with the right leadership, these privateers in the Caribe could be turned into the fighting force that England needs right now to buy time until the Royal Navy and the government can intercede in force."

"Where does Modyford stand on this?" asked Bill.

"We can't really trust any of the Modyfords, you see. The Modyfords are all corrupt," Sir Harold commented. "But maybe just corrupt enough that they might serve our purpose. No, we can't use either James or Thomas. We can't use official channels or the Admiralty. The fighting force is there and, most importantly, already in place. But it's divided between many different nations and interests. What we need is an English captain that could be expendable if the need ever demanded. Some captain who could bring all these different freebooters together under something like a unified command. He would have to be a surrogate, you see. He would be unaware of our true purpose but malleable enough so that he could be directed along the path we choose. You see, William, he would have to be a man that, if the situation turned against us, we could give up. Probably to be hung at the dock as a pirate."

The three men sat silent for a moment as the intent of this devious plan seemed to settle in each man's mind. Bill glanced questionably at his father. He could tell by the look on his father's face that this discussion had already been held and agreed upon by Sir Harold and his father. Bill glanced into Sir Harold's eyes as the man took another drink from the brandy snifter. Bill noticed that Sir

Harold parted his thin pale lips just enough to allow a small sip of the amber liquor to pass between them. The center of the man's wide red-freckled face and receding garnet-colored hair, combed back to cover a brown bald spot at the top of his head, was silhouetted by two thin light red eyebrows that seemed to just dart over his piercing blue eyes. The man's face gave no hint of any feeling or emotion, and Bill could read nothing but alertness in the man's eyes.

It was a bold plan. Enlist an English privateer captain who was well-known in the Caribe and could bring together the other privateer captains in these waters? Well, that would be easy enough for one season of privateering. Mansvelt had done it, of course. Others had also brought together small squadrons of ships to attack both Spanish ships and settlements. But what Sir Harold was now proposing had never been done. A fleet of boucaniers! Men from every nation gathered together by only greed under a captain who the English would condemn at the first opportunity and hang at North Dock as a pirate.

"Which, to ask one question of you, might be one of the purposes of our meeting tonight? Of all the privateers, which one would fit or we could make fit as our surrogate in the West Indies, William?"

Bill thought for a moment before answering. "Edward Mansvelt comes to mind because he has, in the past, gathered together squadrons and fleets of multinational buccaneer captains to attack Spanish settlements. But he is Dutch and is rather too old at this point to consider. Christopher Myngs might be a candidate, but he is also very old and mostly retired. John Davis, as he is called in Jamaica, is an English gentleman of fortune who commands a sixty-ton eight-gun ship and has been a very successful privateer. I'm not sure where he came from before he arrived in the West Indies. Davis is somewhat of a loner and an opportunist. Then there is one of Mansvelt's captains, Henry Morgan. Morgan is English. He also came to the West Indies about the time Admiral Penn and General Venables were leaving. Since then he has taken part in a number of raids on Spanish towns in Central America under Mansvelt and Christopher Myngs. Morgan himself led a raid earlier this year, sacking Villahermosa and plundering Granada. He's a capable leader," Bill said.

Harold Dobbs's actual position within the government was somewhat vague. No one knew exactly what he did, but his father said the rumor was Sir Harold Dobbs was the head of the English Secret Service. This organization collected information for the Crown and developed agents and informants from around the world. Bill's father also had subtle influences both in Parliament and with the admiralty due to connections with Lloyd's and the network of informants that he too had developed over the years as a merchant sea captain in every port of the world. As part of Lloyd's, his father understood that information was the key to a successful business—when to sail, where to trade and whom to trade with, who was firmly in power, and who was being overthrown in a coup. This information he shared occasionally with Sir Harold and other select friends in the admiralty and Parliament where he felt that, in certain cases, it might affect the British interest abroad and did not compromise his own interest. Bill's father had an established spy network that covered every port. He never disclosed sources or how he came by the information that he discreetly shared with his government friends and was always careful to go through back channels such as Sir Harold.

Aside from the information that William's father provided, Sir Harold had his own network of spies that covered a much broader part of the world. Sir Harold had spies in all the dark and secret places of the world. From the back streets of India, China, and into Malaysia he had contacts. He cultivated relationships with the Romanian Gypsies and the Spanish Basque in Spain. From Russia, the Ukraine, France, Germany, Austria, the Netherlands, across the rest of Europe, and down through Egypt and Africa, information came back to Sir Harold.

"Morgan, Henry Morgan, you say?" questioned Sir Harold. "I believe he has a cousin here in England, Colonel Edward Morgan. Edward is a dependable man, from what I have heard. He is a widower, I believe, trying to raise a young daughter on colonel's half pay. He has petitioned the plantation office on several occasions for an appointment. He certainly might be of use to us as, say, a Lieutenant Governor in Jamaica. He would be in a position to keep an eye on Modyford and help us control Henry."

"As a Loyalist member of Parliament, I have friends, William, friends who believe as your father and I do about this matter. These friends extend into the Admiralty, and I have had discussions along these lines of a plan set forth to accomplish exactly what we have been discussing here tonight," Sir Harold said. "William, with your help, we will set this plan into motion. With your help, Henry Morgan will be our surrogate. Edward Morgan, Mansvelt, and Modyford will play the part of the fools in our Shakespearian drama. And you, my son, if you agree to participate in this plot, must never be revealed. While you may direct Morgan and events and most assuredly with my help and your father's very vast network of informants, your success as a privateer is guaranteed, but your role, if you choose to commit, must never come to light. Use this success as you will to gain influence. But your connection with the Crown, my office, or me directly or indirectly or the Admiralty must always remain quieted. You must never, from this point forward, attract attention to yourself. If your ships take a prize, you say it's Morgan who done it. If you command a fleet, it's Morgan's fleet. Morgan and the rest will listen to your counsel because you'll always have information that none other has. And I assure you that you'll have both money and influence."

The logs in the marble-lined hearth were starting to burn brightly, and the dim reflections of the coal gaslights on the walls were overpowered by the flames coming from the fireplace. The three men's resolute faces were cast in shadows by the light from the fire; their crystal brandy glasses reflected the gaslights from the walls as they each held them to drink another sip while the discussion continued late into the night.

"What say you, William?" asked Dobbs as he filled Bill's empty brandy glass. "Are you with us in this plan? Can the Crown count on your services?"

Bill held the crystal glass in his hand, warming the brandy before taking a drink. He smiled at the thought of how this venture might play out in the Caribbean and in the company of scoundrels like Mansvelt, Morgan, and the rest. He realized that Morgan, as the scapegoat in this plot, would be sacrificed. He also knew that if he should ever be discovered, his life would end most cruelly.

"I am your man, Sir Harold."

"Very well then, my son. Now, there are some matters that I have thought of that we might need to put into place before your return. First, while your success as a privateer should provide more money than what might be needed, I will also arrange the issue of £200,000 securities in the form of bearer bonds against Lloyd's, which is common enough to arouse no undue notice. This will assure that you have ample funds at your disposal if needed. Remember that these will be unregistered securities. No records are kept of the owner, and whoever physically holds this paper, in part or in full, may redeem them.

"Second, in order to provide you with some standing among your new friends, I will speak to my old friends at the admiralty concerning your appointment to the rank of Post-Captain, Post-Captain without a ship assignment or duties, of course. This will provide you with both recognition and authority but also allow you the freedom to undertake whatever employment you might find available, being unassigned as it were. And lastly, for your protection and only to be used if the need arises, I will provide you with a letter signed by the King. This document if presented cannot even be questioned by any authority. Even the King's brother, James, who as you know presides as the Lord High Admiral, cannot question this writ. It will state that you are upon particular instructions from the king, and no power will hereby require or demand of you the sight of these instructions that you have received insofar as these proceedings and services to the Crown, nor upon any pretense whatsoever shall you be detained, but on the contrary, you shall be given any and all assistance you may stand in need of towards enabling you to carry the said instructions into execution.

"William, you understand of course that there will never be any official 'instructions' related to this service you undertake? In fact, there will be no record whatsoever, and if pressed, both your father and I will deny this meeting and all that was said here.

"Your post captain's position is and will be a matter of record. Before your return to Jamaica, I will hand you the documents related to your posting as a captain," said Sir Harold. "The other papers are somewhat more sensitive, and we can't run the risk of these documents being found on you in the event that anything were to happen during your return voyage. I am correct, am I not, in the understanding that no one knows of your return to England? All believe that you are still in the Caribbean?"

"That is true, Sir Harold. As my father suggested in his letter, my crew and officers are sworn to maintaining the ruse that I still am present and in command of my small squadron of ships. The squadron may attack Spanish ships in my absence, which would be expected, and to do otherwise would in itself arouse suspicion, but to assure that no loose tongues slip, no ship will make any port until my return."

"Just as well then. For safety, the other documents will be sealed and consigned to an armed messenger ship to be delivered, under your name, directly to the Government House in Jamaica. Might I suggest that your return voyage be most discreet, maybe on one of your father's merchant ships as an able-bodied seaman? Or some other rating that wouldn't stand out. From this point forward, you must be very careful."

A Purse Filled with Gold

28 February 1664, 4:20 a.m.
London Wharf District

London's wharf district was not the Caribe. The smell from the city and especially the river was overpowering, and the cold February sky covered the streets like a damp blanket that wrapped around the city in a gray shroud. Poverty could be seen everywhere. Groups of beggars blocked the narrow streets that twisted between the buildings, where open foul-smelling sewage and raw garbage spilled across every passageway. The sweepers came out every morning and attempted to push the filth either out of the way of the carts or hopefully into the Thames. Pigs ran unchecked through the streets eating the garbage, and rats seemed to control every part of the town. Sections of this part of the city, like elsewhere, had grown unchecked, and buildings abutted next to each other with barely an inch or two gap between each building. And the crowded narrow maze of streets twisted and turned, offering little passageway. There was nothing in the way of any civic improvement, planning, or sanitary system. The rich merchants had long ago abandoned the city and moved to their country estates, leaving London. "No," Bill thought "London's wharf district was not the Caribe."

The street outside Bill's rooming house where he had hidden himself as a common seaman until his father's ship sailed for the Caribbean was filled with men screaming. Seven red-coated brutes with muskets broke their way past the heavy oak door guarding the brothel where Bill slept with three rather chunky young blonde girls. After seeing a play at the Haymarket, Bill had been approached by the girls on the street outside the theatre. The girls said they were actresses and that they were sisters and, in their desperate poverty, offered a rather unique proposition: "Give us food and some shelter, get us off the street," they pleaded, "and then have all three of us as your companions for as long as you like. But only pay a reasonable price for the one you liked the best."

Bathing was not a common practice anywhere in England in 1664. In fact, it was discouraged. So Bill only accepted the girls' offer on the condition that all three girls bathed and burnt whatever clothing they wore. After all three had a brisk scrub in a tub of warm water—probably the first that any of the girls had ever had in their lives—and a new set of clothes from a dressmaker on Jermyn Street, Bill took them back to his boardinghouse along the Thames in the London wharf district. William was working on his second week with the plump ladies, still unsure as to which of the young girls might be the best. He had decided long ago to reward all three handsomely but had not told them his decision. Instead, he just played fun games with the three girls, seeing what each would do. They worked in the theatres as actresses, assimilating any role or character that might be needed in any play presented. Two of the girls were exceptionally smart. They could memorize any script, recite any line with just one quick reading. The third, somewhat less intelligent, was remarkably beautiful, kind, and gentle.

Bill had not slept soundly since he had arrived in London. Day and night, the city noise seemed to ebb and flow outside his window with the clamor of some distracting sound. At night it was just a fitful rumble. About six, the sounds of the sweeps and milk pails echoed against the calls of the merchants. The rumble deepened to a steady roar about nine in the morning with the ringing of London's church bells. Bill was alerted by another noise coming through the background rumble—the sound of heavy footsteps coming up the staircase.

Jumping from the bed, he kissed first one girl and then the next. He quickly gathered what garments were at hand while the three girls watched and dropped a heavy purse filled with gold doubloons on the bed. The purse contained more money than these girls would ever see in a lifetime. There was enough money to take all three of the girls off the streets for the rest of their lives. Throwing his seabag out the window, he jumped from the two-story building. This brothel, like most in London, had no glass on the windows, just shutters, so the thirty-foot fall from the second floor into the foul-smelling street below cost him little but his dignity as he landed lightly first on the balls of his bare feet then rolled forward with the momentum onto his shoulders and back, which cushioned the impact like the compression of a spring.

The men called Marines were actually part of the Duke of York and Albany's Maritime Regiment "of foot" or "afoot," meaning that they did not have horses. They were stationed aboard Royal Navy ships of the line and functioned as press-gangs, gathering seamen for service aboard His Majesty's ships.

While the Marines destructively searched the boardinghouse where Bill had spent the last two weeks for unsuspecting men, breaking everything in sight, Bill, scantily clothed with nothing more than a loose-fitting cotton shirt and white canvas britches secured momentarily at the waist with a single button, picked up his seabag, threw it over his shoulder, and boldly slipped into the crowd. He pulled on his boots as he walked, first hopping on one foot and then the next, seabag over his shoulder. His fingers finally secured first one and then the next of the three white buttons that ran on each side of the boxlike flap that covered the crotch of his pants. His sun-browned face, dark exposed chest under the open white shirt, and muscular shoulders and arms stood in stark contrast to the thin pale-white skin and sunken, hollow dark eyes of the London crowd that stood staring as he ran along the street in the cold morning dawn on his way to the docks.

Captain Mansvelt

21 March 1664, 7:00 p.m.
the Caribbean, 12° north latitude

The weather was warm, and the sky was clear. A brisk breeze filled the sails, pushing the ship through the blue water. Bill was glad to be back at sea. Sailors are, by nature, not wanderers or explorers as some might think. They are always more comfortable aboard a sound, seaworthy ship. Their ship is their home, the sea their country, and the crew their family, and one ship is much like any other for a sailor—safe aboard a home with family. The three-hundred-ton merchant ship was built from the best English live oak that could be found by Blackwall Yard, one of the most reputable shipyards in England. She reached over 150 feet long with a 35-foot beam that gave her ample room for the tons of cargo carried in the hole. Even with a brisk breeze filling the great square sails that hung from three stout masts, she was sluggish and clumsy in the water. With a short keel, towering poop, and forecastle, the ship answered slowly to any commands from the wheel.

After leaving Billingsgate Docks on the south side of the city of London, the ship made its way down London River past nearly a continuous wall of wharves lining the banks and heavy wooden quays that reached out into the murky water. Sailors have a custom of naming rivers after the port it serves, thus the Thames to seafarers is London River. Slowly the ship moved with the wind down the river, finally reaching Chapman Sands near Canvey Island. Breaking out of the river's channel, the helmsman steered a course of south by west after passing the lighthouse into the North Sea. With two days of fair winds blowing south, the ship caught the North African Current, and then with every sail catching the wind, they turned west as they approached Portugal. After a short stop at Ribeira Grande in the Cape Verde Islands to resupply the ship's provisions with fresh fruit and water, the vessel pointed its bow along a latitude of twenty-three degrees due west toward the Indies.

Eight bells sounded. The cry of the lookouts came from around the ship: "Starboard bow, all's well!" "Starboard gangway, all's well!" These were followed by "All's well!" across the rest of the ship. "Eleven inches in the well," Bill heard the man report.

As planned, Bill had signed aboard one of his father's merchant vessels as an able seaman. Crews on merchant ships were not large. Bill was one of the ten seamen onboard. Now thirty days after leaving port they sailed toward the island of Curacao and into the inlet of Schottegat lying at 12° 7' north latitude, 68° 56' west longitude.

The island of Curacao was held by the Dutch West India Company. The town of Willemstad sat on the banks of an inlet called Schottegat. The island offered little in the way of natural resources necessary for plantations or any other island-based enterprise. Nothing was actually produced or grown on Curacao, but it was well situated as a trading port. It was the Dutch equivalent of Jamaica and, like Jamaica, was a contraband port. Merchant ships from all nations came to Willemstad to sell and buy everything that the Caribbean had to offer.

A large bird market floated in the middle of the bay on a wooden platform covered by faded orange canopies, under which brightly colored birds were sold to passing ships. There was an amazing selection of brightly colored parrots; snow-white cockatoos; scarlet, blue, and gold macaws; large green beaked, black and yellow toucans; various kinds of raptors like the black harpy eagles and ospreys; kingfisher birds; mangrove cuckoos; and parakeets. Some of the birds were able to say words in French, Dutch, Spanish, or English. They were bought mostly as bribes offered to officials at other ports. Trading vessels of every description rested at the busy docks, some loading cargos that had been purchased, others unloading their cargos to be sold.

Bill made his way along the crowded docks, ducking into several taverns, looking for Catlina. On entering the Het Dode Paard (the

Dead Horse) Tavern, he knew that he had found the right place. Dasha splashed across the floor of the Dead Horse Tavern in her favorite bright lavender skirt and loose blouse that was held in place by a dark burgundy silk corset that rested firmly, just as she liked it, under her perfectly shaped teardrop breast and was then tied at the front with long black ribbons. The bottom front edge of her ankle-length dress was pulled under the broad leather belt cinched tightly at her waist, exposing her brown legs from underneath the folds of lavender petticoats as she danced. Red-laced, black leather high-heeled Spanish riding boots clung to the sweating calves of her shapely legs under the folds of the dress. Perspiration also soaked her light cotton blouse, revealing two wet, stiff, erect dark nipples that sat centered on firm brown breasts held suspended above the corset. A damp red scarf wrapped around her head held her long shoulder-length black hair. Limp black strands of wet hair clung to her forehead in tangles just below the raw red edges of the cotton band that covered her head. Dasha enjoyed dancing. She enjoyed the looks of the men in the crowd and the shouts of excitement as they watched her dance. The pleasure that she seemed to bring to them as she twirled captivated her. She enjoyed the attention. Much like a moth to a flame, Dasha always came back to these taverns, where she danced for her enjoyment at seeing men swoon over her. Even kill for her on some occasions.

Sweat dripped down her back, ending wetly at the base of her coccyx, that remnant of some long-forgotten vestige of a reptilian tail that, in another life, Dasha would have probably been comfortable with. Her wet, bare thighs clung to her lavender skirt as she twirled.

A few in the crowd that night might have noticed Bill as he entered the tavern. Most in the room that night saw only Dasha. Some taking a second glance might have even seen a stunning lady approach this man and throw herself into his arms. But most were just watching Dasha dance.

Holding Cat in his arms, Bill discreetly glanced around the room, placing the faces he recognized with names and questioning those he did not recognize. Willemstad was a rough town with rough, hard men. "Cat, my love," Bill whispered in her ear as he kissed her passionately. They held the embrace and the long wet kiss as Bill picked her up off her feet and spun her around in a wide circle.

"Walker, you bastard," she said, smiling, pushing coyly away from his tight grasp. "You leave me too long alone, my love. I have almost forgotten you. A woman like me doesn't wait for any man. Men wait for me."

"Then if you have forgotten me, maybe your cousin Dasha will better remember our times together."

"Beware, William. I'll have her eyes and yours if you bed her without me. She is a young toy, a toy that we both can enjoy. You truly are a bastard, William. But I still love you."

Bill and Cat found a table and ordered rum. Dasha, finishing her dance, pranced toward the table. "Walker!" Dasha shouted in delight as she glided across the room and placed herself on his lap. "Walker, my darling man, you have been absent from my bed far too long." Her warm, wet lips and tongue explored Bill's mouth as she kissed him.

Looking up Dasha shouted across the room, "Alexandre!" A young well-dressed man of medium build and height standing at the bar turned in her direction and smiled at the Gypsy girl. He walked to the table where Bill, Cat, and Dasha were sitting, a pint of Kill Devil in his hand.

As the man approached, Dasha whispered into Bill's ear, "This is my new lover, William. He's not as good as you, but I have been teaching him how to please me."

"Dasha, my love," the man said as he crossed the room to the table.

"William," Dasha stated, "may I introduce Alexandre Oliver Exquemelin. You might want to know this gentleman. He is usually with a cutthroat Dutchman that ports out of Tortuga. Alexandre, may I introduce to you Bill Walker."

Both men acknowledged each other formally by tilting their heads downward, slightly in a nod. Bill's left hand rested on the hilt of the dagger hidden under his coat at the center of his spine.

"Alexandre is an old Huguenot who was reportedly run out of France and now claims to be a surgeon," Cat added. "He thinks that he can win Dasha's affections. And if his money lasts, he might just do that."

"Monsieur Exquemelin, my pleasure," Bill stated.

"What brings you to Curacao?" asked Exquemelin.

"I'm looking for a passage to Jamaica."

"Can you help him, Alexandre?" Dasha pleaded.

"It may be possible, if you don't mind the company," said Exquemelin, smiling. "The Dutch pirate that is so fondly spoken of is Edward Mansvelt. I ship with him and a crew of hard men notorious for their foul language, heavy drinking, and casual violence. And he is in this very port and intends to sail on the tide for Jamaica. The devil will play at any unholy game, it seems. And Mansvelt is the devil's own work. So, my friend, we truly are 'sailing with the devil,' as some say about pirates and the like."

Alexandre then turned and shouted, "Master Boot, another round of Kill Devil for my friends and I!"

Nicolaes Boot was the proprietor of Het Dode Paard Tavern. He quickly moved through the crowd to the table accompanied by his young daughter, Margaret, both ready to provide whatever service the gentleman might request.

"Where is Captain Mansvelt now, Alexandre?" asked Bill.

"His ship docks alongside the pier, loading supplies. We'll pay him a visit as soon as we've finished these drinks, and maybe another," Exquemelin said, smiling as he pulled Dasha into his arms.

The company at the table had not only the next round but another after that, a serving of roasted pork and bread, and then another round of Kill Devil to end the evening. Dasha was called back to the dance floor, and Bill, promising to meet Cat later, followed Alexandre out of the tavern and along the dock to Mansvelt's ship, the *Rover*.

"Captain Mansvelt, I found this Englishman onshore in a tavern, and he wishes to join us on our voyage to Jamaica," stated Exquemelin on entering the captain's cabin.

"Captain William Walker, sir," said Bill as he entered the cabin behind Alexandre.

"Walker!" exclaimed Mansvelt as he approached Bill, recognizing him at once. "By my word, and where else but in this godforsaken place, Bloody Bill himself it is. Don't you know who this is, Alexandre?"

"Just another down-and-out mariner?" said Exquemelin. "He sailed into Curacao aboard some English merchant carrying a cargo."

"We sail on the tide, my son. Come aboard at dawn."

"By the way," Bill asked, "is Morgan with you?"

"Aye, Morgan be with me," replied Mansvelt. "I believe he's ashore someplace getting drunk with some wench."

Bill made his way back to the Het Dode Paard Tavern, where Cat led him upstairs to her room.

"I have a surprise for you, my love," she said as they stood just outside the door to her room. "One that we can both share."

Opening the door, Cat led Bill into the dim candlelit room, where he saw young Margaret, Boots's daughter, lounging on the four-poster canopy bed. The girl was smiling. Her bright blue eyes were dilated. Long limp blond hair fell across her wide chest and broad shoulders. Two tiny strawberry-red erect nipples protruded above a cushion of soft white flesh that folded gracefully into the curves of her plump body. A green onion-shaped vessel of rum and a tray of moist coca leaves sat beside the bed.

"Maybe this will take your mind off Dasha," Cat stated in a low, quiet voice.

Recruiting a Crew

4 June 1664, 6:00 p.m.
the Blue Goat Tavern, Port Royal, Jamaica

Prize Money

£ Hundreds £

Captain Bloody Bill Walker, hero of the Dutch wars, master mariner and famous navigator, captor of the Dutch galleons *Standvastigheid* and *Herlige Nacht*, who in his fabled ship *Commencement*, has pursued many capital voyages in the West Indies, who has vanquished the foes of His Sovereign Majesty with great capture of rich treasures and vast booty, has berths for good men and crue on his ship *Commencement*, a 10-gun Dutch costal trader of great power and speed, fitted out and victulled with attention to the comfort and care of the officers and men. Those seamen who have the good fortune to sail under Captain Walker on his previous voyages have shared prize money as much as £200 each man.

Sailing under letters of marque issued by His Majesty Charles II (God bless him!) Captain Walker will seek out the enemies of His Majesty in the ocean of the West Indies, to their confusion and destruction the winning of rich prize of which one-half to be shared by offers and crew.

All good seamen seeking employment and fortune will be heartily welcome to take a pot of ale with Big Daniel the quartermaster of the *Commencement* at the Blue Goat Tavern, Port Royal June 4th 1664

Big Daniel stood over six feet four inches tall and weighed over eighteen stones. He was an extremely strong Scotsman with an unusually small head that sat atop his thick, muscular neck. Braided and tarred long red hair hung to his shoulders at the back of his head. His ruddy red face spouted a large blue-veined nose that had been broken many times and large moist pink lips. Daniel had "rounded the horn" and, by tradition, wore a single small gold hoop earring hanging from his left earlobe, the ear facing the cape while sailing east. He sat with several other mariners in the Blue Goat Tavern by a corner window at a large round table, filling their pewter mugs with rum from wide, flat-bottomed, dark green–colored glass bottles shaped like large onions. The shape of the container was a result of the needs of the tavern owner, who wanted a more stable bottle, which was less prone to tipping over and breaking. Crimson sunlight passed through the dirty beveled-glass windowpanes and splashed across the table dimming the oil lamps being lit in the darker cloisters of the tavern's interior.

It would be another season of privateering in the Caribe, and a new crew had to be recruited. Big Daniel had placed the posters across the island of Jamaica wherever seamen were likely to gather. Finding good sailors wouldn't be a problem. Most would be turned away. Only the best, most experienced with the special skills needed would be signed on under articles of agreement for this venture. Unlike the British Royal Navy, who sent press-gangs of armed men ashore or boarded merchant vessels at sea to indenture both sailors and landsmen alike, privateer crews were all handpicked volunteers. Sailors in port and at sea were always at peril of being impressed to service by the Crown's Navy because harsh discipline, poor living conditions, and low pay on board navy ships never attracted enough able-bodied seamen to fill the vast number of vessels needed by the English to carry on one war after another with the French, the Dutch, and the Spanish. An ordinary seaman in the Royal Navy only earned eighteen shillings a year. From this were deductions for the Greenwich Hospital, the chaplain, the surgeon, and the Chatham Chest. And too many Captains held a seaman's wages until the end of a voyage to discourage desertion. With a single Peso worth four Shillings and sixpence, four silver reals in the hand of a common seaman would be more than a year's wages. A single doubloon could easily amount to more than a man could earn in three years. Impressment of seamen became legal and authorized by the Crown. On most naval ships, half the crew was forced into service, and mutinies were not uncommon. The few Royal Marines, who were all volunteers and well paid for their service, were placed on board warships primarily to prevent mutinies. Naval battles at the time were fought at a distance. Standing back and firing large cannons at the opposing vessels rendering them to splinters, the red-coated Duke of York's Maritime Regiment afoot were there to enforce discipline on board ships and impress whatever seaman or landsman that could be found ashore to man the Royal Ships of the Line. The Duke of York's regiment were called Marines, and they wore the distinctive red coats and blue trousers that distinguished these men from the blue coats and white britches worn by the navy or the red coats and white trousers of the army.

The mariners that came into the Blue Goat that evening were a different breed of men from landsmen. They walked with a swagger-like rolling gait as they moved across the floor, and their faces and arms were burnt to weathered nut-brown leather. They wore short blue jackets over checkered open shirts and long canvas trousers held in place with wide leather belts with brass buckles. Some wore red waistcoats and had scarves loosely tied at their necks or wrapped tightly around their head. Most wore buckled shoes that ended just above the ankles, and they spoke a different language that those not familiar with could hardly decipher.

"Ho! Bloody Bill sails again, does he! To harry the Spanish with a pretty bill for the dons to pay, says I. 'Ere he comes back again!" Daniel shouted. "Into the Caribbean, shipmates, for the Spanish popist bastard's ships that carry the wealth of nations in one vessel."

"And the share?" asked another at the table.

"As the notice stated, me lad, one-half be for the crew," answered Daniel. His large, meaty scarred hand grasped a pewter tankard of rum and brought it to his lips. "Seventy to one hundred stout-hearted lads is what we seek. One-half, being crew's share, will set the likes of most of you in good keeping for a while if you don't drink too much and your whores aren't greedy."

"And the ship, Daniel, is it a good ship, commander, mates, and crew?" sounded a young man named Mathew Riley, who stood nearby. The young naïve boy asked the only questions he knew to ask, the ones that his mate on the merchant vessel had told him to always ask before signing on to a ship. "Is the captain lucky? Is it a happy ship?"

"Aye, mate, it's a lucky ship," replied Daniel. "It's a seaworthy vessel if there ever be one, and sound as oak she is, says I. Cap'n Bill only takes worthy hands on board, berthed and victulled solely for the comfort of the crew. On that you have my affidavey. Just like being in your dear mother's arms, sailing on calm waters with the gentle waves rocking you to sleep at night in your hammock."

"My mother was a Bristol whore, she was. And I care not to see the likes of her again," one of the sailors said, laughing.

"We love you all the more, Mate Roberts." Then addressing the young bright-faced sailor at the table, Big Daniel said, "And have no fear, Mathew Riley. The Spanish wouldn't dare harm a child as pretty as yourself."

The other men at the table laughed, and the young man blushed.

Daniel called for more rum. Turning back to Mathew, hoping to restore his confidence, Big Daniel said, "You're young, my lad, and coming off that merchant vessel as ye did after the Spanish attacked ye, well, that's a true marvel for any man. But you're smart. I seen it first off. Bright you are, bright as a polished brass button, says I. No, my lad. No common English sailor are ye with little hope of anything in your purse. Like the rest of us you be looking for more."

"But, shipmates," shouted Daniel, taking another drink of rum and standing, "who among ye are lucky? Lucky sea dogs who fear nothing? Who among ye has the sea chosen worthy to sail upon her breast, ask I?"

Daniel and the other sailors in the room believed that the sea was a living thing. These sailors believed that the sea had the ability to determine whom she felt worthy or unworthy to travel on her. But as Daniel looked around the tavern that night, he saw some in this crowd he considered unfit for either land or sea.

"What the sea wants, the sea gets, says I," stated another from the crowd in a gruff baritone voice.

"Aye, lads. That be true," Daniel admitted, squinting one eye and turning his head in the direction of the gruff voice that came from a one-legged, toothless old man standing next to the window.

"I seen it rounding the Horn, I have. If you ever kiss her cold, icy lips, she'll have ye. I've known both men and ships pulled from her cold embrace that lived on only borrowing time, as it were. If the sea wants ye, she'll take ye soon enough."

"The Horn?" questioned the young boy Mathew. "What is the Horn?"

"Who has not heard of it? Cape Horn and a horn indeed, that has tossed many a good ship. Drake made it. He crawled his way through the gales and rounded the Horn."

The number of sailors around the table grew, listening to Dannie's story. And more came through the open door of the Blue Goat in groups of two or three shipmates at a time, pushing their way to the table. The atmosphere livened as more rum was served. Young smiling bar girls loaded down with heavy pewter tankards danced their way nimbly through the crowd to the lively harmony of a six-hole diatonically tuned fipple flute, a fiddler, and the hollow blend of the paired string three-octave hammered dulcimer playing salty-aired melodies in the background.

"The Horn, lads, makes a brave man braver, but far less daring after ye been around her. Ye may approach soundly from this direction or that, in any way you please. From the east or from the west, with the wind astern or abeam or on the quarter, and still the Horn is the Horn, and it will take the conceit out of any freshwater sailor and will steep the saltiest among us in even saltier brine. Woe betide the tyro, the foolhardy. Thirty-two days it was, my first time round. Thirty-two days of cold, freezing sea and winds. We hung the heaviest storm sails from short rigging on only two masts that bent under the weight of the freezing rain. The winds changed, and we had to take in sail. The top reefers were sent aloft. As they climbed into the rigging, the williwaws fell over the ship. Men's hands and toes froze to the ropes. Aye, lads, we cut frozen blue fingers and a blue toe or two away just to get the men down from the rigging."

"Williwaws?" one man around the table questioned skeptically. "I heard it all now."

"Aye, it's a wind it is. A wind peculiar to the forties and those latitudes about. Cold air builds up behind the steep slopes of the high Andes and then suddenly spills over the mountains with a great splash into the sea. It rolls across the water with the speed of a hurricane. The wind is like an invisible iceberg. Woe be to any boat caught in her path. The Horn is impracticable, it is."

The men around the table sat silently, listening.

"Heaven preserve!" came a solemn voice from the crowd.

"But enough of me sea stories, mates," Dannie announced to the men gathered around. "The *Commencement,* lads, it's Bloody Bill's ship, and he's a flower of the flock, Bill is. There's more gold resting discarded on the decks of that ship than are in twelve mates' pockets tonight."

Gold…! The word hung over the room like an apparition and was whispered quietly around the table.

"Gold!"

"Mansvelt is a man too. So is Davis by all said," another commented.

"I never sailed along with neither, but by all accounts, Bill might be the better. Where's all Mansvelt's and Davis's crew? I dunno. Why, most of 'em aboard here in this very tavern tonight are glad to get the duff, but sadly, most have hung or are under the hatches, all said the same they be gone."

"Gentleman of fortune we are. We live rough and risk swinging on the gallows, sailin' under a captain without the respect of the Crown and letters. But if we sail fair, we eat and drink like fighting cocks, and when a cruise be done, why, it's hundreds of pounds in our purse. Albeit,"—he laughed—"most goes for rum and a good fling under the covers with a dandy young wench, and then it's back to sea again for us. Time enough on shore too, says you. Aye, but if you have a crown, a mere five shillings, then live easy in the meantime, never denied o' nothing that your heart desired, and sleep soft in a young woman's arms and eat dainty. But then it's back to sea for the likes of most of us, it is."

"Sic erimus cuncti postquam nos auferet Orcus ergo vivamus dum licet esse, bene," stated a well-dressed man in a white open-neck silk shirt that was covered by a long brocaded coat of blue wool that dropped almost to his ankles, hiding the slim French rapier hanging at his side.

Daniel's head turned toward the man; he recognized him at once. It was Captain Brossard.

"Meaning all respect, sir, what popinjay nonsense is that, Captain?"

Brossard grabbed the nearest bar girl passing next to him, pulled her into his arms, and kissed her. The girl dropped the heavy tray that was suspended above her head and melted into the Frenchman's arms.

"For you, my lord, a florin. Only two shillings and I'm yours."

"It's Latin, Dannie," Brossard announced. "You being an educated man, quartermaster, ye are that and more by my sounding. But the words mean 'If the devil is going to take you anyway, then live well in the meantime.' Live well while you can, live well before he takes what is his by right, your soul and destiny. And the devil will take all of us in the end, you know. "Sic erimus cuncti postquam nos auferet Orcus ergo vivamus dum licet esse, benem," Brossard said again as his coated figure disappeared into the crowd.

The bar girl followed at his side, begging, "I can be yours, my lord."

"And right ye be, my lord. Live well before the devil takes us all, it is!" Big Daniel cried in a heavy voice that carried into the street outside the tavern. "Come, Mathew Riley, drink a toast to the devil. More rum! Rum and plunder, me lads! Rum and plunder!"

The Blue Goat Tavern was a drinking house, a gambling parlor, and a brothel of the first order that only tolerated gentlemen of the highest esteem. There were no drunken brawls or killings at the Blue Goat, or very few, and the young girls were the finest in Jamaica coming right off the captured prize vessels and the slave and prison ships that sailed into Port Royal almost weekly. The owners of the Blue Goat purchased from the auction blocks only young, lighter-skinned, large-breasted Negro and Arab women from slave ships; dark-haired, almond-skinned Spanish girls with big brown eyes coming off captured Spanish vessels; blond haired, English and red haired Irish girls with blue eyes, small breasts, and large hips from prison ships; and there was also the occasional white-skinned, dark-haired, plump-breasted, slim French girl that came up for sale.

During these years in the Caribbean many girls made their fortune or fame in places like the Blue Goat. And some after a few years working in these taverns either married rich landowners in the colonial Americas or returned to England or France as prosperous ladies. For a captured girl of fifteen, no matter the race, working at the Blue Goat for a share of her labors was a better chance at life than the alternative of endless slavery on a sugar plantation or an indentured servant or prisoner with no hope for freedom and no monetary reward.

As Mistress Helen, the madam of the Blue Goat, had once explained to Bill, "You can't make money with a slave whore. Without pay, the girl's heart won't be in it. She'll offer no pleasure to her customers. It would be little more than mating with sheep, and the riches that pour into the Blue Goat Tavern are unbelievable. Why, there's more money in Port Royal than in the whole city of London! And most buccaneers pride themselves on spending every last piece of eight they have plundered within a few days. What would have amounted to a life's fortune is often gambled, drunk, and whored away within a few days ashore. So the girls get a share, and well worth it, I say."

With the crowd that Daniel was bringing in tonight with barrels of raw-rum and free drinks and the hope of signing on for a voyage with prize shares, the girls in the tavern and Helen were doing well tonight.

Cristy danced nimbly through the crowd of sailors with the drink tray held high above her head, hips swaying to the music. Her white pinny was wrapped around her waist and tied in a bow at the back. Her young freckled face and ample charms had caught the attention of many, those and her low prices. As she glanced around her adopted home, she saw women for every taste—from the cool flowerlike Creole, quadroon courtesans whose rich lovers treated them better than they did their own wives as long as their mistresses' bloom lasted, to jolly young Cristy, who would take whatever she was offered. There were women to be bought whatever your purse, she thought. Cristy always had a kind word, a smile, and the overt suggestion of more pleasurable company upstairs to all hands. She hoped that at least some of Daniel's recruitment fee for the crew he was enlisting would find its way into her purse by morning.

Cristy was not to be disappointed. Coming down the stairs from her room, she saw the tall, thin, young black-haired rector, Reverend Stearnhurst, of the Church of England, who cherished a nip now and then and appreciated the warmth of a young repentant girl seeking God's salvation in his bed. He was drinking in a corner of the tavern, watching the entertainment. Christy appreciated the fact that the reverend did not inveigh his congregation with fiery oration against drunkenness, fornication, sodomy, or most of the other cardinal sins. Instead, he preached sermons about salvation and God's forgiveness.

The tall blonde native girl with the tattoo on her arm sat next to him. It was rumored that this girl had been placed in his care by a Portuguese slave trader, and most in this crowd had seen the girl many times before because the reverend was a frequent visitor to the Blue Goat, and the girl seemed to go everywhere that Stearnhurst went.

"Coin well spent," she flattered herself as she came down the stairs from her room. Still holding the florin from her last customer in her hand she smiled as she reached the bottom of the stairs. "And coin well-earned I might add."

A Dandy Young Wench

5 June 1664, 6:00 a.m.
the Blue Goat Tavern, Port Royal, Jamaica

As the morning sun was just peeking through the mist-covered harbor, Cristy brought Daniel a pot of freshly brewed dark Jamaican coffee ladled with dark brown raw sugar and sat beside him at the abandoned table. She held his calloused hands for a moment and then stood behind him and started rubbing his thick neck and shoulders. Where once the tavern was lively with sailors drinking and singing, now the calm of a new day settled into the quiet background of the empty bar.

As the sun rose the off-shore breeze called the doctor's wind came across the island. The cool sweet sea air carried away the smell of rum, tobacco and the heavy sent of unwashed bodies that mixed with perspiration and the lingering aroma from fornication that hung in the air of the tavern. Even though Cristy had been upstairs many times during the previous night, her perfume, which she used liberally after each client, overpowered the tavern's smell. Daniel breathed her scent into his lungs as she leaned her heavy breasts over his shoulders, her strong fingers working the superficial and deeper layers of muscle and connective tissues across his broad back and neck as she massaged him tenderly. Adam sat down at the table with his ledgers.

"Cristy, me darling! Ye a comfort to an old man."

"Dannie!" she sighed, dropping off the last sounds as he pulled her next to him. "My dear man, you may be an old fool, but you're not an old man, and I would welcome you in my bed at any time. As my guest, I might add," Cristy declared as she leaned over him and kissed his forehead. As a guest, Daniel would not pay for her services as the other sailors had done that night.

"And that blessing I will enjoy as soon as I tend to Adam and our new crew."

Cristy left the table and walked up the creaking wooden stairs to the second floor and down the narrow hallway to her small but comfortable room. She was looking forward to spending the day with Daniel. In her mind, she planned what would happen. First they would make love, which she would actually enjoy, and then they would sleep as the cool, light breezes of the trade winds that are born five hundred miles away in the Gulf of Mexico came through the corner windows of her room. They would wake in the afternoon, have coffee and an embrace, then attend the Anglican church services. Maybe go into the mountains and bathe in one of the springs that formed deep, refreshing pools along some of the riverbanks. Maybe have dinner at one of the many local establishments in the cool foothills of Spanish Town. Then hopefully at the end of the day, she looked forward to but a single client and a comfortable bed with Daniel.

Christy sang to herself as she removed her dress. She poured water from a lime green pitcher into a matching ceramic bowl, adding crushed jasmine petals to the water, and, with a sponge, bathed her body. Setting the sponge aside, she stood nude at the window. Lifting her arms, she pulled her hair back onto the top of her head, and singing, she twirled like a marionette on a string in the morning light.

With one hand holding her long blond hair on the top of her head she closed her eyes and as she sang she moved her other hand slowly across her moist, supple strawberry nipples. She reach down past the round indented navel, where a thimble of jasmine-scented water still pooled, and then across her plump white belly. As the cool breeze blew across her wet body, slowly her fingers crawled to the warm, moist, downy plum between her legs. Christy heard Daniel's footsteps coming up the stairs and down the hall to her bedroom.

And You A Gentleman

6 June 1664, 1:00 p.m.
the Blue Goat, Port Royal, Jamaica

Bill climbed the stairs to the hallway on the second floor. Inside his room, he changed his clothing and then walked down the corridor to Cristy's room, where he knew he would find Daniel. The door to Cristy's room was not bolted, and Bill walked into her room. Cristy and Daniel were still asleep, the rose-colored bed linens pushed to the side; Cristy was lying sprawled across Daniel's chest, her plump round ass and chubby short legs uncovered to the afternoon sun that was coming through the open window. Bill pulled a chair beside the bed and put his hand on Cristy's firm butt, shaking her awake.

In a quiet voice, he said, "Cristy, my dear, can you spare Daniel for a few hours?"

She rolled over, only half-awake, moist eyes only half-open. Startled, she pulled the sheet across her breasts and legs.

"Cap'n!" she declared. "And you, a gentleman, unannounced in a lady's bedroom." Breathlessly, she shook the man lying next to her. "Dannie, wake up!" she pleaded. "Cap'n is here."

The open windows allowed cool air inside the small room, but sweat beaded Dannie's brow, and the perspiration-soaked mattress clung to his back as he lifted his head off the pillow. The few lingering smells from the bed that were not covered by Cristy's perfume were not pleasant, and he wondered how many other men had lain here before him.

Daniel drew himself up and sat on the edge of the bed, pulling Cristy into his arms, trying to cover both of them with the thin, damp sheet. He said, "We have the crew, Cap'n. Sound men all, they are. Where's the ship?"

"She's in the hole, where she put me ashore in the skiff. You and Cristy go back through the tunnel to Shark Grotto and take the skiff back to the *Commencement*. Then sail to North Dock and set anchor. Have Adam get the new people on board at North Dock," Bill said.

"I'll have none of those dark caverns, Daniel," Cristy interrupted. "They're filled with bats. You go about the Cap'n's business, and I'll meet you at North Dock."

"Be still, my child," Daniel said to Cristy, and then he turned to the captain. "Aye, Cap'n."

Bill turned briskly and walked toward the door of Cristy's room. "Cristy," Bill stated turning his head back toward Dannie and Cristy. "My love, you will always be a beauty that fills my heart with joy,"

"Walker!" She exploded. "How dare you. And you, a gentleman."

William said as he walked towards the door of her room. Closing the door behind him, he walked down the hall to the narrow staircase leading to the floor below.

"Cristy," Daniel said after Bill had left the room, "come with me! We can leave Port Royal."

"Where would we go, Dannie? In the end, Dannie, your life is in the cap'n's hands, not mine. It be different. I would feel different, and I would go with you anywhere as long as we were together. But you're not mine, you're the captain's," she softly said as she stood beside the bed. She walked to the table where the ceramic basin and pitcher sat, poured freshwater into the bowl, and purged her plump armpits, thighs, and under her large hanging breasts with the wetness that was held in the porous cellular mesohyl cells of the sponge.

Governor Modyford Arrives

6 June 1664, 7:00 p.m.
King's House, Port Royal, Jamaica

The governor's mansion had been moved from Spanish Town to Port Royal after the English took Jamaica. The mansion in Old Spanish Town both had a better climate, being farther back offshore and into the elevated foothills of the Blue Mountains, and was a larger, more regal estate with several acres rather than the cramped three-story stone dwelling that sat on High Street pressed between the Admiralty Court and Fort Carlise. But all the British governors insisted on a residence in Port Royal, where they could be assured that no graft slipped through their hands. Every ship that sailed from or came into Port Royal paid the governorship a fee of 3 percent value of the cargo. The governor also issued letters of marque to any and all privateers at a higher fee of 10 percent of the prize before shares to the crew and the Crown, but for that fee they also expedited the provisioning of powder and other arms needed for the venture.

Mary Elizabeth Morgan had arrived in Jamaica with her father, Edward Morgan, four months earlier. Edward Morgan had been appointed Lieutenant Governor of Jamaica, just as Sir Harold had predicted. Although Bill had seen the young sixteen-year-old Mary Elizabeth Morgan on every opportunity possible, she still captured Bill's attention when he first entered the sitting room of the governor's mansion that evening for dinner. She was wearing an extremely low, off-the-shoulder neckline, white satin baroque bodice with paned elbow-length sleeves lined in burgundy and a matching ankle-length pleated petticoat. The scooped neckline displayed a décolletage of bare skin that hovered a fine line between proper and sexually unsuitable for a girl her age. She was tall, long-legged, and slender and had a head-turning physical presence about her that radiated a childlike innocence and at the same time hid a shadow of sublime lustfulness. Her cinnamon-and-cream complexion set off bright amber eyes that sparkled in a healthy, youthful glow under perfectly arched heavy brown brows. Her shoulder-length auburn hair was worn in a mass of tight curls; she wore pearl eardrops and a pearl necklace that hung suspended between the folds of her small, swelling white breasts. Her low-heeled white shoes were tied at the instep with an elaborate burgundy ribbon rosette.

"Captain Walker!" exclaimed the lieutenant Governor, standing and walking toward Bill as he stepped into the room. "I am happy you could join us this evening." Edward took Bill by the arm and led him into the crowd of guests gathered that evening to meet the new governor and for the usual round of drinking, dining, and discussions of the Crown and matters of the West Indies colonies. Schemes, counterplots, and deals were connived and put into place during events like this and were the real purpose of the gatherings.

"Captain Walker, you of course remember my daughter, Elizabeth. Elizabeth questions me about you constantly," the lieutenant governor said.

"Captain," she said in a light, throaty voice as Bill kissed the back of her hand, "it is a pleasure to see you once again." Her bright, catlike amber eyes fixed on Bill's as she rose from her fashionable, just-perfect curtsy. "As Edward has said, I so want to see more of you. However," she added, "the dashing sea captain, it would seem, has other duties that take him away from me."

"Elizabeth spends much of her time now at Sir Thomas Modyford's new plantation in St. Katherine's Parish," Edward Morgan noted. "Port Royal isn't really the place for a lady. Our new governor is coming from Barbados. Have you been to Barbados, Captain Walker?"

"I believe I stopped off there a few months ago," Bill answered.

"He sent his brother, Colonel James Modyford, ahead with five hundred convicted Irish felons from English prisons to build the estate on two thousand acres. I believe he plans to plant cacao."

"Do you know St. Katherine's?" Elizabeth asked.

"I have been through there many times," Bill replied, absentmindedly thinking back to the meeting he had had with Sir Harold and his father in London. *So Modyford's bribes were allowed to go forward, and Sir Harold has his man as governor in Jamaica*, he thought to himself.

"Then you most certainly must visit me there," she said excitedly. "We will call the new plantation Sixteen Mile Walk. That name was my idea." She laughed. "And both Thomas and James loved the name. Rachel, my maid, and I are choosing all the furnishings, draperies, and colors and setting out the household. Each week a new ship arrives with furnishings and china for the estate. It's so exciting!" She giggled. "We have fifteen carpenters, twenty stonemasons, and two hundred slaves building the plantation house. I am told that Thomas is using ironwood framing and heavy blocks of limestone cut from quarries nearby for the house. Everything is so grand. Please, come and visit me."

"I will make myself available to your wishes at any time," Bill responded, still holding her warm hand and smelling the scent of her perfume that rushed into his head as she stood next to him.

"Captain, let me introduce you to our other guests," said the lieutenant governor, and they moved away from where Elizabeth was sitting.

She didn't talk to Bill or seem to be aware of him the remainder of the evening, which allowed him to contemplate her from across the crowded room. Though he had been in her company many times before, he was always captured by her youth and beauty as if it were the first time he had seen her. She was a willful, spoiled, physically attractive young girl that Bill thought he would like to try and tame. But tonight he had other concerns, and she would have to wait.

"Governor," said Edward, "may I introduce Captain Walker." Edward then moved along to his next guest, leaving Bill and Modyford alone.

"One hears much of Walker and his conquest," replied Modyford. A very expensive gray wig with tight curls that reached to his shoulders seemed to hold Modyford's white, pasty powdered face in an ugly smear of misshapen features. Bill noticed that the sweat from his blue-veined, porous nose had melted the thick white arsenic powder, and now the bulbous nose seemed to dominate his face. The man's weak, limp crystal eyes stared into Bill's. "And of course, his fight against the Spanish. How do your plans set today, Lieutenant Walker?"

Bill's face turned red, and his voice suddenly rebounded in anger to almost a shout. "It's Captain Walker, sir, as you well know. I handed my papers of appointment to your secretary personally. And if you are not completely out of touch with the admiralty, then you had also received notice of my commission."

"I beg your pardon," Modyford stated, smiling. "Captain, you say? Maybe I did see something. Walker? Yes, I believe that your name did come up. I'll try to remember."

William remained silent.

"My commission, young captain, and my instructions from the Crown are to, among other things, prohibit granting any further reprisals against the Spanish, and in fact, I'm to encourage trade and maintain friendly relations with our Spanish neighbors. So your well-intended services as a private man-of-war may not be called for in the future. But we can discuss that some other time. It is a pleasure meeting you tonight…Captain, is it? I look forward to our acquaintance. By the way, any venture that you might propose to undertake out of Jamaica will now require my hand to any letters of marque or instructions authorizing any venture."

"Thank you, Governor Modyford. I look forward to a mutually beneficial relationship."

William moved farther into the crowded room. Seeing Henry Morgan, he walked in his direction. Morgan stood surrounded by three middle-aged women all fawning over him, listening attentively at his every word.

"Captain Morgan," Bill interrupted.

"Captain Walker, my pleasure to see you again," Henry responded. "Ladies, may I present Captain Walker."

Walker bowed and kissed the hand of each lady as Morgan recited their names.

"And if you ladies would be so kind as to excuse Captain Walker and I for a moment," Morgan asked the ladies.

The three women giggled, curtsied, and moved into the crowd.

"As you know, our mutual friend is back from Tortuga, and we meet tonight in the Cathedral," Bill said quietly.

"The large chamber in the caves beneath Port Royal," Morgan stated. "Yes, I have heard of the place, and I'll be there." A cunning smile crossed his face.

"And Modyford has just rescinded my previous letters of marque." Bill walked with Morgan across the room.

"Don't worry. At this point, it seems to be only a formality. However, Uncle Edward did happen to mention that our new governor sent letters to the president of San Domingo expressing his intentions of fair cooperation and cessation of hostilities before he left Barbados. Edward also informs me that Modyford is planning to send the *Swallow* to Cartagena with similar letters to acquaint the governor there with his new policies. But as always, we'll do as we like."

After a somewhat joyless dinner, where Bill was seated between two flamboyant middle-aged women with dyed red hair, of obvious intent and sexual interest not only in Bill's touch but also in each others, William said good evening to Lieutenant Governor Edward Morgan, Governor Modyford, and Henry Morgan and started to walk out of King's House.

Elizabeth floated in his direction, leaving her other male companions and admirers standing in a cluster of confused rejection and disappointment. "Captain Walker, my darling." Almost like a cat, she rubbed her body next to his. Unbelievably, a deep audible purr coming from somewhere inside her carried the words to his ears. "I believe that you have been ignoring me this evening." She breathed heavily and glanced coyly into Walker's eyes as they stood on the steps of King's House.

"Never in life would I ignore someone as beautiful and dear as you, my lady," Bill said as he kissed her young moist lips; her tongue played inside his mouth.

"Then we must meet again—as suggested." She slyly sighed and pulled momentarily away from his touch. Then bringing her lips to his ear, she whispered, "And soon, somewhere, somewhere less crowded hopefully, where we can be freer to better know each other." She pulled back from his arms and stated in a stronger voice, obviously intended for other ears, "You had promised to visit me. I'll look forward to that promise." Leaving him, she bounced back up the stairway into the governor's mansion.

Captains of the Coast

*6 June 1664, midnight
the Cathedral, Port Royal, Jamaica*

The arched stone ceiling in the underground cavern called the Cathedral was so high Bill couldn't see the top through the darkness as he looked up into the shadows above. The crystal calcium carbonate tips of the stalactites seem to hang suspended in the black night air, reflecting the candlelight from below like so many stars in the sky. Hundreds of thick candles blazed in elegant brass sconces across the open chamber of the cavern. Two large chandeliers hanging from massive chains hovered in the black sky at the center of the room above a massive rectangular wooden trestle table. Looking down, he could see that the cavern's limestone floor was worn so smooth that it resembled polished marble and over the years had taken on a rich golden-brown patina. Smaller tables consisting of nothing more than wooden planks set atop large barrels and draped with wide ribbons of red cloth were set about the room. Some of these tables were covered with bowls of exotic-looking fruits; others cradled pipes of wine, kegs of beer, and rum. Others held heavy silver platters of smoked meats and fresh raw fish sliced razor thin. Mounds of boiled pink-shelled crabs and shrimp were spread across one table. The orange glow of candlelight also illuminated a treasure trove scattered haphazardly in the cloistered nooks and crannies of dark recesses inside the chamber.

Bill noticed large oil paintings encased in heavy gold-gilded frames, sea chests filled with bolts of Chinese silk, unusual silver, and gold Aztec and Inca artifacts, medical and navigation instruments, and very old-looking leather-bound books. This particular atrium within the cave system under Port Royal was surprisingly dry and maintained an even temperature of sixty-two degrees year-round. The low humidity and constant temperature made this an ideal storage room for plunder.

But it was the people that attracted Bill's attention as he walked into the chamber. Not just a few, mind you, or a dozen, but perhaps as many as forty men and women were scattered around the chamber, each face silhouetted briefly by the flickering glow of candlelight and then hidden in the next moment by a shadow of darkness. Some stood around the tables in small groups, eating; some were sprawled out on chairs, drinking; and some stood lingering in clusters around the room, talking. All held goblets affixed to their hand like they were a part of their bodies, a seemingly natural appendage. The laughter of girls and the shouts of men mixed subtly with the hush, quiet, secretive voices of conspiracy all echoing off the walls, blending pensively with the eight-foot-pitched plucking strings of an Italian harpsichord as it played one of Byrd's compositions.

The men dressed in silks and velvets were by far as flamboyant in their style as most of the women. Bill saw captains dressed in black velvet trousers and jackets, crimson silk stockings, and white taffeta shirt, collars embroidered with colorful silk patterns.

David Marteen, the Dutch privateer, stood talking with Anne Dieu-Le-Veu, who wore a black open-neck velvet shirt with gold lace and crimson silk britches that hugged her narrow hips. Both must have come out of Tortuga, Bill thought. If Anne was in the room, then Pierre Length, her new lover, must also be somewhere close, Bill speculated. The stunning red-haired beauty, Jacquotte Delahaye, a French-Irish woman privateer, stood almost naked in a long white high-neck, see-through Chinese silk dress, slit up both sides past her hips. The gossamer material clung to her body like a mist from head to toe, momentarily revealing long brown legs as she moved fluidly across the room to Lieutenant Brossard. The bare diaphanous brown-and-white figure languished momentarily in Lieutenant Brossard's arms. Jacquotte was known as Back from the Dead Red. It was said that she had once used voodoo to escape the gallows by faking her own death. *Brossard had best be careful with that woman*, Bill thought.

The British captains John Morris and his son, John Morris the Younger, mingled among the crowd. Captain Freeman stood alone, gnawing a leg of roasted lamb while the juices ran down his face and onto the crimson coat he wore. Young Calico Jack, displaying his brightly colored burgundy coat, white shirt, and navy blue velvet britches, flirted with some dark-haired tavern wench. Most importantly, Bill spotted Robert Searle, better known as Captain John Davis, standing in a dark corner away from the light, wearing a black velvet doublet with gold buttons, his hand resting gently on the gold hilt of his saber. Laurens Prins, the Dutch buccaneer often called Prince Lawrence, was talking with Bernard Claesen Spierdijk, better known as Black Bart, another Dutch privateer out of Curacao who commanded the eighteen-gun *Mary and Jane.* Standing with Black Bart was another Dutchman, Roche Braziliano. The Spanish called Braziliano the Roach, and the name had stuck. The Roach sailed out of Tortuga. Two English captains, Daniel Johnson and Lewis Scot, both also out of Tortuga, stood together with a group of young ladies. Daniel was often called Johnson the Terrible.

Bill recognized the Hawk. He was also known as John Hawkins. Bill had learned that the man's real name was Richard Sawkins. This John Hawkins was not the famous Hawkins that had sailed with Drake. The Hawk sat at the table in the center of the room with Mansvelt, Morgan, and Moise Vauquelin, an old Jew from Normandy who had been around the Caribbean for as long as Mansvelt. Christopher Myngs, however, was not at the table, nor did Bill see him in the room. Myngs, John Morris, and Morgan had sailed on many a privateer venture together, and the fact that he was absent was disheartening. Myngs was either a strong supporter or a fearsome enemy. There were other captains in the room that Bill recognized, but these few men that he had looked for were the ones who would pull everyone else together.

Old, bearded, pompous Mansvelt seemed to be the unquestioned senior spokesman for the group, and as Bill approached the table where he sat with Morgan and Hawkins, Mansvelt stood, removed his cock-plumed, wide-brimmed black hat, bowed toward Bill's general direction, and without a word, the music stopped, and the meeting seemed to have been called to order. The other captains pushed for space and chairs around the long table. Marteen, Morris, Freeman, Davis, and Calico Jack easily found chairs as the others deferred to their status. Mansvelt sat at the head of the table. Morgan sat on

Mansvelt's right, and The Hawk sat to his left across from Morgan. John Davis stood in the dark, away from the light, his hand resting on the crown of his saber. As agreed beforehand, Bill stood back from the crowd and was not seated at the table.

The three-week voyage from Willemstad to Port Royal aboard Mansvelt's ship had given Bill ample opportunity to discuss his plan of a unified privateer fleet with Mansvelt and Morgan. Mansvelt immediately grasped the concept and agreed with the idea. Morgan came around to the idea days later as Bill and Mansvelt spent hours in the captain's cabin discussing the plan and refining the details. Morgan's relationship with the governor was an essential factor. Bill did not disclose Sir Harold's part in creating this concept or any details surrounding an English involvement or separate deals that might be offered to Morgan at a later time. It was agreed that Mansvelt would be admiral of the new privateer fleet, and Morgan, with Mansvelt's backing, would be appointed vice admiral. Bill's role was to guide Morgan but stay in the background, letting Morgan take all the glory or blame, as the case might be. Mansvelt would support all of this and manage Morgan and the other captains as long has he got the lion's share of any prize.

"Captains," Mansvelt said. A still hush fell across the room as Mansvelt's voice echoed around the rock walls. "Brothers, we are in these waters and captains of ships that sail these seas. We sail where we wish and take what we will. These coast and lands are ours for the taking. We are brothers in these waters, brethren in these seas, along these lands. No country claims our allegiance. We are brethren of these coasts."

The term *brethren of the coast* was not something new that Mansvelt had thought of independently. It had been in use since 1640 around Tortuga. But the statement was something that every Captain in the room could identify with. And it seem to have an alluring ring to it. Knowingly or unknowingly, Mansvelt had just pulled together this band of scoundrels into a group.

"Brethren of the coast," he said again, letting the phrase settle into each man's mind. As with any good leader, Mansvelt knew that he had made that very important first connection with his audience. Not wanting to let that moment pass, he raised his cup in a toast, and the men at the table and around the room did the same.

"To us!" he shouted. "Brethren of the Coast!" they all replied and drank from their cups, repeating over and over again the mantra in a cheering chorus. "Brethren of the Coast!" all shouted.

The girls standing by the table poured more rum, ale, or wine from large decanters and jugs as the case might be to fill each captain's glass. Cristy, from the Blue Goat, came to Bill's side, filled his glass, and kissed him on the cheek.

"Mon ami," she whispered into his ear as she poured wine into his glass. "If you need me, I am here."

"French now? I like it, my love," he said, pulling her closer to him and kissing her wet pink lips. "French women are always the best lovers, you know."

"They certainly carry the most diseases," she callously whispered into his ear.

"But, my love, what you don't understand is that fornicating with French women is not so much a pleasure as it is an obligation, a duty bestowed on every English male," he whispered into her ear as she pulled away from him and slipped back into the dim reaches of the candlelight.

"Captain Henry Morgan has a proposal for us and a means to carry out that plan. There might be little risk compared to your other ventures, and the rewards could more than compensate for those risks," Mansvelt announced. "Captain Morgan, if you would kindly explain your proposal."

Morgan stood and laid out a sheaf of papers on the table. "Recently, I have come into possession of a number of documents, a sample of which I bring tonight, that detail Spanish fortifications and armament at various ports. I also have in my possession detailed sea charts of these ports, soundings, currents, and navigational directions to enter and leave any Spanish harbor. The Spanish treasure galleons are becoming harder and harder for a single ship, a single captain, to capture. Now we capture more merchant vessels than treasure galleons. The Spanish convoys sail past beyond our reach, and if or when we happen to capture a vessel, we have to sell our booty into limited ports and at half the value. The Spanish coast is still rich, but now the seas are protected by Spanish warships, and the real wealth evades us. No longer can we individually seize that prize Spanish nao treasure ship laden with wealth.

"I have talked to captains that sailed and fought in the Mediterranean against the Moorish corsairs. I have studied these campaigns. These corsairs attack ships and the coastal settlements in fleets under one command, like the British or French Navy's. They then sell their spoils collectively into the highest-paying Arab bazaar. As a group, they are unbeatable, and they profit with every venture. In fact, at one point in history, every European nation has paid tribute to these Moroccan and Algerian pirates. What I propose is that we, Brethren of the Coast, do the same as the corsairs. I say we band together collectively in a fleet of privateers. Together we can take what we want and then collectively sell our spoils into a port that pays the highest price."

Morgan's enthusiasm mounted as he explained "his" plan, and his deep voice echoed off the vaulted ceiling and around the walls of the cavern as the group of mercenaries sat silent.

Bill smiled as he listened to Morgan's speech and saw the expressions on each face at the table. "He's doing it, Cristy. He's got everyone at the table interested," Bill said to Cristy, who stood next to him, her warm, moist hand holding his as he looked across the room into the silent crowd.

A few of the sea charts that he had captured from the Spanish ship and the diagrams of some Spanish castle that he had stolen from the admiral in Havana was what Bill had given to Morgan. These documents were shifted around the table, eventually coming in front of each captain as each individually examined the sample maps and blueprints.

While the shuffling of papers was still going on, Morgan announced with pride, "And I have informants already positioned at most of these Spanish ports who can tell us everything we need to know that is not contained in these documents." Of course, Morgan actually had none of these things. It was William Walker who had the informants, the sea charts, and the details of all the Spanish port's fortifications.

"Why, with ten ships and five hundred men, I could take almost any port I choose," Morgan bragged. "And most importantly, if we all held back our goods and sold collectively, we could name our price in port.

"But before discussions go further, we must agree upon certain articles, as it were, between captains, which are put in writing, by way of bond and obligation, which every captain who joins our community is bound to observe and all of those set their hand to. Therein, we specify and set down very distinctly a single code between brethren captains, which all recognize and subscribe to. We form articles, agreements, a contract; if you please. A code unique to our business. Each captain will then sail with his own crew, under his own flag, and establish his own articles with his crew, outside of what we do here tonight. Tonight we determine the course for the future." Morgan then sat down.

As Mansvelt stood, Bill whispered to Cristy, "The articles between captains was Mansvelt's idea, and a good one, I think. Those that survive outside the law must be assured of honesty between themselves."

"Something to think about? Aye, gentlemen, something to think about. I now ask that you each think of our future, your future," Mansvelt said. "Drink and eat your fill. There are women handy nearby, and consider what has been said. Those interested, come back to this table within an hour's time and pledge your support. Those not inclined, go your way."

Mansvelt turned a large hourglass over, and the sand at the top of the glass started to sprinkle gently down into the lower chamber. A ship's bell rang three times. The harpsichord picked up a lively note in the background.

When the white sand had finally run through the hourglass, Mansvelt signaled, and the ship's bell rang again. Twenty captains came back to the table. Adam, the scribe and linguist from Bill's ship, was already drafting in quill and ink on parchment the first part of the contract in his distinctive, expressive, and harmonious style of script. Twelve captains were British. Morgan was first, followed by Hawkins and Marteen. Morris and his son came to the table next. Freeman followed. The French and Dutch captains followed the English.

Adam had already written *Chasse-Partie* in bold lettering across the top center of the long cream-colored goatskin parchment page. And under that heading in smaller letters, he scribed the words "Jamaican Brotherhood Codex and Custom of the Coast."

The next few days were spent in chaotic meetings with groups of the Captains in the Cathedral. William had met with Mansvelt and

Morgan privately, and using what intelligence he had gathered from his spies and what Sir Harold had sent him, he quickly organized a sequential list of targets that offered the best opportunity for easy success. It would be important that this first campaign undertaken by the newly formed brotherhood be both successful and rewarding. Therefore, two separate squadrons were formed and each fleet given a list of plump, easy targets. Adam made copies of what was needed, and each captain was given all the fortification plans, nautical charts, men, and provisions that they needed to be successful. Without formal letters from Modyford, it had been agreed that, if questioned, they would claim that they had Lord Winsor's instructions that had been previously issued. If just one of the two squadrons were successful, then it would come down to just how greedy Modyford was and not a question of legality.

The Island

7 June 1664, 7:30 p.m.
the Caribbean, an Unchartered Island

The *Commencement,* under the command of Lieutenant Cribb, set sail with the morning tide from North Dock. The Blue Peter flag had been hoisted, and cannon fire announced her departure, calling all hands. Adam and Daniel went through the town gathering up the recruits. Mathew, the young sailor, and one hundred other new crewmen had staggered or were carried limply onto the ship, where each drunken sailor found a place on the open deck where they could lie down, and all quickly fell into a deep, rum-soaked sleep. A few sober hands managed to raise the anchor and set one sail. By the time the blurry-eyed, hungover recruits sobered up, the *Commencement* was well out to sea with Big Daniel at the helm running the ship westward. The crew was rousted by the order to "Come about, course south by southeast," issued by the grave voice of Lieutenant Cribb. This new course would take them toward the hidden island.

Mathew and the other men moved quickly about the deck and up into the rigging, dropping more sail. Now with a steady breeze under full sail against a clear blue sky with waves slapping against the hull, the ship ran briskly between the many dots of land that crowded the sea along their way. Most of these islands, Mathew noticed, were fringed with coral sand as dazzling white as snowdrifts and crowned with thick dark green vegetation, over which slender palm stems curved gracefully into the sky, their tops shaking in the gentle trade winds. Hundreds of white-plumed seabirds flew overhead, feeding off schools of fish that stretched for leagues in all directions. Schools of fish like yellowtails were so densely packed together that they slowed the passage of the ship as the bow pushed through them. Pods of twenty-five to thirty smiling dolphins swam alongside and at the prow, leaping from the water in brilliant white flashes. Coming closer to the uncharted island, Mathew thought he saw the figure of a young girl riding one of the dolphins as it ducked below the water.

Big Daniel called Mathew to the wheel.

"Mathew, my lad, take the wheel in your hands, and I'll show you how to steer a course," Daniel said.

Eight bells sounded from the small belfry below the mainmast.

Mathew, taking the ship's wheel in his hands and with Daniel's instructions, threaded the ship into the narrow passage through the clear green waters where shoals and reefs lurked darkly beneath the surface like massive malevolent monsters ready to bite into the ship's fragile hull.

"Hoist the ensign," ordered Lieutenant Cribb. And a red-and-black pennant crawled up a line to the top of the mainmast, where it unfurled and blew briskly in the breeze that came offshore. Gun crews on the island, seeing the red-and-black flag at the top of the mainmast, let the ship pass.

"Take her in," Big Daniel said to Mathew. "Take care now of the tide race as we enter the channel. Steer just starboard. Now, lad, feel the current pushing against the wheel as the rudder ropes tighten and watch the bowsprit sail. The foresails will catch the wind. Keep her pointed at a close reach two points off starboard and drift her gently into the flow."

The *Commencement's* shallow draft allowed her passage into the channel between the treacherous coral reefs that protected the hidden island, her hull unmolested. Under Mathew's hand, the ship's bow cut through the green water into the cove just before nightfall as the tide receded and the water calmed over the bay. Entering the lagoon at sunset, the hidden bay turned into a mesmerizing display of burnished copper splashed with glimmering translucent streaks of orange and red sunlight.

"Turn the wheel now sharply to drop her down, below the mark," Daniel quietly said.

Mathew spun the wheel to leeward. The sails, losing the wind, began to flap, and the sheets hung limply from the yardarm while men crawled into the rigging to reef the sails. The vessel glided gently to rest in the peaceful lagoon. As sails were tied to the yardarms, the anchor rattled loose from the cathead. A plume of gushing white sand erupted from the seafloor as the anchor came to rest. Brilliant colored fish scurried left and right to escape the intrusion of the heavy iron anchor. A large brown octopus turned magenta and propelled its way away from the ship into the clear turquoise blue water. Several flounder lifted their flat bodies out of the white sand and swam slowly away. Looking over the taffrail at the leeside of the quarterdeck, Mathew thought he saw several unclothed brown women leap off the backs of dolphins and swim for shore.

While Lieutenant Cribb secured the ship, torchlit longboats trudged down the river from the settlement into the lagoon to carry the new recruits back to the shelter of the island. Leaving the ship and rowing from the lagoon into a blue stream, Mathew was surprised at what he discovered as the boats pulled ashore at the wooden dock alongside the river. Under the shadows of the tropical foliage overhead and the scattered light from the fires and torches spread around the encampment, Mathew and the new crew discovered a hidden primitive paradise.

William had long ago realized that while Port Royal might be a good harbor for supplying and refitting the individual rogue ship, it wouldn't be suitable as a hiding place for his small squadron if for any reason he and his men had too disappear. Quite by chance, Bill discovered a chain of uninhabited coral islands and cays that, like Jamaica, had been borne from undersea volcanic eruptions and earthquakes occurring millions of years ago. Within this cluster of small uncharted islands, he chose one island that was about eight miles long and four miles wide. It covered an area of about twenty-five square miles. At the western end of the island, mountains rose to a height of five hundred feet. A river ran from the mountains through rolling hills toward the east; one branch of the river ended in a mangrove forest and a swamp, and the other wider branch ended at a sheltered lagoon. Because of the coral reefs and shallow sandbanks that surrounded the little island, few mariners had ever landed there. The island's hidden cove offered a deepwater anchorage that was well protected. The lagoon was also difficult to navigate into.

Bill knew of the Frenchman named Le Vasseur, who, sometime in 1642, together with a company of fifty other Frenchmen, made a surprise raid on the Spanish Ile de la Tortue or Tortuga, so called because of its turtle shape, off the north coast of Hispaniola. The raid was successful, and Le Vasseur declared himself governor of the small island. He built a strong fort and armed it with cannons. He called the fort Dovecote, and the only way to reach it was by means of steps cut into the rock and iron ladders. So under Le Vasseur, Tortuga became a prosperous buccaneer settlement and the headquarters for many of the more unscrupulous sea rovers of the Caribbean. However, La Vasseur was eventually killed by his own men in protest to his paranoiac harsh treatment of those around him. But Tortuga continued to prosper to this day as a buccaneer stronghold.

Using this example, Bill hoped to do the same with his island, but in secret. He began diverting everything that could possibly be of value from captured prize ships he and his crew had taken onto the island. Many times he towed or sailed the empty captured ships back to the island so that they could be dismantled piece by piece and the salvaged wood, fittings, rigging, and canvas then used onshore. The island had no name and was always just referred to as the Island.

A Privateer Port

13 February 1665, 5:00 p.m.
King's House, Port Royal, Jamaica

The town of Port Royal was still celebrating the return of the privateer fleet in a frenzy that could only be appreciated or could only be known or imagined in a place that was called the Wickedest City in Christendom. Fortunately for Morgan and the other captain, both campaigns had been extremely rewarding, and the privateer ships brought their booty from their six months of raiding back into the protected harbor of Port Royal.

The *parliamentum* to writing the first Codex and Custom of the Coast started in the Cathedral. It would take months of continuous editing and refinement to complete. The wording and the language that had to be used to satisfy all parties was a compromise. Most of the document was a mix of Latin, French, and Old English. But in some places, where an agreement could not be settled on, Adam very cunningly embedded Hebrew and even Arabic words that no one knew the exact meaning of. Over the many years that followed, there were many interpretations of what some parts of the document actually meant and what was intended. But in the end, this first edition not only established written rules, laws, and guidelines that all agreed to follow, but also established the mechanism of a Brethren Court to hear complaints and grievances, render verdicts, and pass judgment in cases where captains went against the code. No one at the time would ever have guessed that this singular document would be adopted and used for the next one hundred years by the most ruthless gang of brigands ever to set sail on any sea. And no one would ever know that Thomas Jefferson would pull wording from this document to write another document over a hundred years later that announced the independence of the colonies in the New World from English rule.

Doubloons, pesos, and jewels, spilled from every buccaneer's pocket and were spent without regard in every tavern, brothel, and gambling house that the city had to offer. Each crewman had received at least the equivalent of 250 English pounds as his share from the six months of raiding. Jewels and precious stones were hard to measure or determine the value of and handfuls of red rubies, green emeralds, uncut diamonds, and black pearls just floated from one hand to the next around the bars and whorehouses. For any man, this was a small fortune that, spent wisely, would have lasted him the rest of his life. "Rum and plunder!" they sang as the wonderful Port Royal girls of all ages, colors, shapes, and sizes flaunted themselves in the streets and taverns as if they were untamed, wild, feral creatures as much addicted to strong drink and lustful lascivious living as any man coming off a ship with a purse.

And the girls were all too willing to share a sailor's good fortune if the price be right. The celebration of Morgan's return would last uninterrupted, both day and night, for more than a month until each man's money finally ran out. Oddly, considering everything, the four churches at Port Royal were just as crowded most mornings as the streets, brothels, taverns, and gaming houses had been just a few hours earlier. The offering plates that the tall blonde-haired girl collected as she passed between the pews of Reverend Stearnhurst's Church of England spilled over with pious donations from sinful men and thankful women.

What arrived at Port Royal at the end of the venture was supposed to have been all that had been taken, but from the beginning, only half the treasure made it back. Much of the gold and silver had been concealed and unaccounted for. Modyford would never know about this part of the treasure and would never have the opportunity to take the king's and the governor's share. But even with half the booty that made its way back into the governor's hands, it was a substantial amount that everyone was pleased with. It was such a fantastic amount of money that no one could imagine that there could possibly be more. Modyford had unfortunately arrested the first few captains that sailed back into Port Royal with their holes packed with captured Spanish merchant goods. In a rage, he had charged the men with the crime of piracy, and one poor fellow had actually been hung before Lieutenant Governor Morgan could put a stop to it.

Captain William Walker was greeted by Mary Elizabeth and two black servants as he entered the door to the governor's mansion on High Street. It had been a bright cloudless day in the tropical paradise of the West Indies, and Bill's trip from his hidden island back to Jamaica had been uneventful. He had arrived the day before, and as was his custom, he stayed at the Blue Goat Tavern despite an invitation from Lilly to have dinner with her at King's House. He chose instead to drink rum at the Blue Goat downstairs with the other patrons of the establishment that were still celebrating the success of their last venture and the lively entertainment that Helen, Cristy, and the other girls provided.

William didn't like these open meetings with Modyford. Sir Harold had frequently warned him about any overt involvement with King's House and the governor. "Let Morgan do the talking. You control Morgan and stay in the background," he would say in his messages. But today, Morgan had insisted that Bill attend this meeting.

Entering King's House, Lilly ran across the room and kissed him warmly on his lips as she pulled herself into his arms. He could feel the pounding of her heart as he held her close and looked into the black pools of her dilated amber eyes. She was filled with excitement and joy at seeing him again, and her young, nimble body responded knowingly to his touch.

Henry Morgan interrupted the interlude. "William!" he shouted from across the room. "William, the governor and I have been awaiting your call. Come now. Let's not delay." And he took Bill by the arm and led him into the governor's study, where Modyford impatiently sat behind his desk reading a letter, and Colonel Edward Morgan sat quietly in a chair by the Governor's desk.

"His Majesty cannot sufficiently express his dissatisfaction at the daily complaints of violence and depredation against the Spanish by ships out of Jamaica," he read aloud with a bright red face. "Again," he skipped down in the correspondence. "I strictly command not only to forbid such violence and depredation...etcetera...I command, in the king's name, that all privateers are to return to port and no further letters of marque be granted or issued." There he stopped and threw the paper onto his desk.

"Morgan! You, Walker, and those other thieves I have in jail, Morris and Jackman, say you were operating under the old letters of marque? The commissions granted under Lord Windsor, not any orders approved by me. You sacked and plundered Villa de Mosa, Rio Garta, the Port of Truxillo, and the city of Granda." Taking a glass of ale in his hand, Modyford glared at Henry Morgan for a response, but Henry, intimidated by the governor's outburst, sat silent. "And now I receive this letter in response to your actions! I told you, Morgan, and you also, Walker, that all previous letters of marque were revoked. Did I not?"

Both Morgan and William sat silent as the governor continued his rage.

"And along with it I have another letter from the admiralty that states England and the Netherlands are once again at war. I suppose I am to fight the Dutch without bloodshed as well!" he shouted.

A hush fell over the room. Then Bill started to speak softly.

"As you realize, Governor," William stated calmly, "the political situation in Europe and the Caribbean is somewhat volatile as it concerns Spain. Remember, the Black Death has devastated London and continues to be a problem. Now fires spread throughout the city. The king has sought safety from the disease and is no longer even in London. England is not at war with Spain and has no intention of declaring a war. She can't. But her interests here in the Caribbean are certainly threatened by the Spanish. And while Charles might have to denounce you occasionally, officially, and publicly in response to Spanish claims in the European court, what do you think is your real purpose as governor in Jamaica, and what do you surmise are the real wishes of Charles? England and Europe after all are quite a bit different politically and far distant from the Caribbean. And you cannot expect the king or Lord Arlington to know what is in the best interest of a far-flung colony in the West Indies. As you well know, the real differences between England and Holland actually have nothing to do with us. It's about the East Indies, not the West

Indies, that they fight over. Decisions about the West Indies, my dear Modyford, rest in your very capable hands.

"England is at war with the Dutch. There is no question about that. Charles sent the navy this very year and seized the Dutch settlement of New Amsterdam in North America. The Lord High Admiral, Charles's brother James, renamed the city after himself, New York."

Everyone in the room understood that when the House of Stuart and Charles II gained control of the throne of England after the death of Cromwell and the collapse of the English Commonwealth, James became the Duke of York.

"Governor, the question you must concern yourself with is, will France as Holland's ally follow? And if France sides with the Netherlands, how will that affect your situation in the Caribe? Let me ask you, if the buccaneers are not allowed to dispose of their booty and refit their ships when they come into Port Royal, where might they go? And let me assure you, Governor, these Captains of the Coast will continue to plunder these waters. They will run contraband out of any port. They will defy all countries. You don't have the warships to stop them, and no one else does. So where might they go, to the free port Dutch at Curacao or the French at Tortuga maybe? And then without Port Royal as a haven and a place to sell their goods, these buccaneers, who might remain loyal to English interest, are free to prey on Jamaican and British commerce."

Modyford stared inquisitively at William but said nothing as a thin smile crossed his lips.

"If, on the other hand, you were to adopt a more conciliatory attitude to retain their allegiance, these buccaneer captains would offer the handiest and a most effective instrument for driving the Dutch, the French, and the Spanish out of the Indies. You, my dear Modyford, would have the navy that you so desperately need to protect Jamaica, at no expense to the Crown, and then take credit for their deeds or disavow their actions, as the case might be and you choose. After all, these privateers would not be directly under your control. And if one scoundrel should happen to exceed the letters of marque and instructions that you provided them? Well, you deny any culpability. In the meantime, untold riches would find their way into Port Royal, each taking his share. It's all for show, my dear Modyford. It's all for show. Do you think that Charles would want to stop the flow of gold that comes out of the Caribbean? Gold that supports his throne? If we are now at war with the Dutch and possibly the French, then you send ships refitted at Port Royal and captains under letters of marque only against the Dutch and the French. Spain? If a few Spanish ships or towns are plundered along the way, then you disavow any knowledge of these actions, and perchance if Spanish booty happens to come back to Jamaica, then all the better for Charles. Let Morgan worry about the details," Bill said, turning to Henry.

"Yes," stated the Lt. Governor. "Let my cousin worry about the details. But we must assure that the privateer ships that come into Port Royal are welcomed and supplied with powder and shot and that their captured prize can be sold here at a profit outside of what the Dutch or the French will offer, and without too many questions."

"And, Governor," Bill added, "Please, no more arrest, and certainly no more hangings. You jeopardize the entire island if you continue taking such harsh actions."

"An open privateer port is what you're asking? An open port that offers the best prices for captured goods?" Modyford asked frowning.

"An open merchant port where the Crown and the colony and the governor profit by undercutting taxes on captured goods. But by charging less, we bring in more, so we make more in the long run," commented the lieutenant governor. "But, Thomas, think for a moment. If you and I were to enlist the aid of the merchants in Jamaica to outfit privateer ships coming into port as, say, an investment instead of the Crown's direct involvement in these matters? And further, let's say if in someway illegal booty did find its way into Port Royal, with of course no knowledge of the governor? And these merchants claim the booty as their share of the investment? The Crown would be in no way involved. The government's share is then taken from the merchants instead of the privateers. Goods sold on the open market and a fare tax. Charles still gets his third, and the governorship takes ten. The privateers and the merchants both still prosper because every privateer is guaranteed, without question, a market for their spoils. Thomas, raiding settlements and capturing ships filled with treasure is the easy part. Any brigand, highwayman, can do that. It's selling it that poses the problem."

"Enough!" Modyford shouted. "What of this Dutch war? I am being directed to strike against them."

"The Dutch?" Bill queried. "What would hurt the Dutch most in the Caribbean? The Dutch have never been much in the way of plantation owners or empire builders. Remember that the Dutch charter in the East Indies, the Vereenigde Oostindische Compagnie [United East India Company] as elsewhere is not controlled by the government. It is a purely commercial interest. They have realized the strategic importance of trade and placing neutral ports in between islands owned by different competing colonial powers. There is Curacao, St. Eustatius, and St. Maarten as examples. These free ports are neutral trading points that the Dutch control that break the dependence of the colonial islands, trading only with their mother country. Harass these key Dutch ports and you would interrupt the flow of commerce throughout the New World and cripple the Netherlands. It would also bring trade back to Jamaica because the Spanish don't have free ports. Dutch ports are the key, not Dutch ships. Cripple the Dutch ports and everything that once went into these safe havens is now destined for Jamaica if it is a free port."

"The Spanish interests in the New World are strictly controlled by their government, and merchants have little to do with their policies. The Spanish are empire builders. Their weakness is their plantations and their treasure galleons.

"And our weakness," questioned Moydford. "What is England's weakness?"

"Our weakness is our resolve to do what is necessary" answered Edward Morgan.

"Then, gentleman," Modyford said in frustration, "I leave this task to you. Port Royal will welcome any legal privateer with papers into her port that does not attack or interfere with British interest. Whatever might happen behind my back? Well, I can't be responsible for, can I?"

Modyford and Edward Morgan left the room, leaving William and Henry Morgan behind.

"What do we do now?" questioned Henry.

"We, Henry," William responded to his question somewhat belligerently, "bring together whatever English ships and crews you can find to attack Curacao and St. Eustatius. We, Henry, will also then look for Dutch or French ships and captains to capture the island of Providence or what the Spanish call Santa Catalina, off Colombia, which tactically holds the key to further English ventures in the Spanish Main. That island will become our new staging point for our ships. From there, we can attack Spanish settlements along the coast. And, Morgan, my friend, if you ever hope to be admiral of the brotherhood, then you must start acting like one."

William stood and stormed out the door of the governor's study, leaving behind a bewildered Henry sitting seemingly hopeless in a comfortable chair in front of the governor's desk. William burst through the doors of the study, into the foyer, and made his way determinately across the pine-planked floor toward the door.

"William!" Elizabeth called as she followed Bill down the wide steps leading from the porch. "William! William!"

Bill turned and caught her as she tossed herself lightly into his strong waiting arms. Her long brown muscular legs wrapped around his waist, choking the breath out of his lungs. And she kissed him, a kiss with a moist, wet open mouth that tasted of honey. Her long, auburn hair shrouded his head in a haze of brilliant translucent sunlit colors. That amazingly youthful, healthy animal hunger that she possessed overpowered his reasoning, and he was no longer mad at Morgan or anyone else. Now he only lived in that one moment for her.

Pulling her hair aside with her hot, moist breath still against his face, he saw glistening beads of light perspiration covering her bare arms and shoulders and felt the dampness between her trembling brown legs that wrapped around him tightly in the hot, humid afternoon. Her wet open mouth and tongue played across his lips and face and down his neck, devouring his soul with each mouthful she took. And at the same time she breathed life into him with each heavy, pure breath from her lustful young lips. She made him vulnerable and compliant to anything that this girl wanted but he knew that he had to leave her.

"I have to go,", Bill told her and stepping from the porch of King's House onto High Street he walked a few blocks then turned to the right and walked long James Street, which would take him back to the Blue Goat. The public market was empty except for two platform pillories that held some petty crooks. Both seemed to be asleep. Along the narrow confines of the muddy cobblestone path of James Street, where the celebration was still in full swing, Bill pushed his way around bare-breasted women fornicating with sailors along the roadside and past open shutters from rooms on the second floor of the buildings lining the street, where naked women, recognizing him, called as if sirens beckoning to him to come to them.

Bill waved to each girl and called their names in a cheerful greeting but continued walking. A drunken sailor perched on a keg of rum sat in the middle of the street, blocking his passage. The man had a pistol in each hand, and two dirty, mud-covered nude women sat at his feet. The man encouraged—no, threatened—all passing to drink with him.

"Come drink, my friend, and have your pleasure with these fine women!" he shouted. "They're already paid for."

Looking at the two young drunk girls, Bill obliged the sailor, taking only a drink, and after finishing his cup and looking again at the women, he declined the offer of the girls and wished the mariner and his ladies a good evening. Dim orange-colored lights spilled from the taverns' windows and doors, and music and singing from inside the taverns filled the avenue briefly; then the sounds and lights faded as he walked past each establishment. Bill stepped over the bodies of drunken sailors and discarded young girls as he walked toward the Blue Goat. Some of these inebriated souls lying about the street, if not already dead, would be dead by tomorrow's sunrise, and the governor's men, leading carts, would pick up each body out of the mud and dump them into the sea. Bill had known of some who had been picked up by the carts and dumped into the sea who were, in fact, not quite completely dead and, by some miracle, swam or floated back to shore.

As he came to a narrow alley, a woman approached him, coming secretively from the shadows.

"My name is Rachel, my lord."

The woman handed him a folded paper secured with a red wax seal and the stamp of the letters *ME*. The woman's black beady eyes looked at him from under the shadow of a wool cloak that covered her head and body. They were the eyes of a predator—bright, alert eyes but without any glimmer of warmth. When the envelope left her hand, she turned quickly and ran back toward the dark alley where she came from.

Bill placed the envelope discreetly in his pocket, unread, and walked down the street. He entered the front door of the Blue Goat, walked up the stairs to his room on the second floor, and locked the door behind him. He withdrew the letter that the woman on the street had given him, broke the red wax seal, and examined the note.

> *My Dear Captain,*
>
> *In March, God willing, I will be at Montego Bay. I plan to lunch and stay for a while—alone. My hope is to be at this beautiful place for a week. My thought is of you and your ventures, which you must tell me of.*
>
> *If it is in your heart, you can join me there.*
>
> *I am yours, hopefully,*
> *Lilly*

Bill folded the letter and placed it in his pocket. As he made preparations for the meeting with the captains in the cathedral, a brief thought of Elizabeth's slender, young body lying on a white beach crossed his mind. "Enough of that," he told himself as he closed the door to his room behind him. Without a second thought of the girl Bill walked out the back door of the Goat toward the cellar and into the hidden cave entrance.

After the meeting with Modyford and Morgan at King's House, Morgan sent word to Mansvelt demanding that he bring what captains were available together that evening in the Cathedral. Most were still in port, celebrating, and were available. Catlina and her father, Diego, had their Gypsy camp at Isla de Providence and were sending messages by carrier pigeon to Bill weekly. For Young Dasha, William had placed her along with a large sum of money in Het Dode Paard Tavern on Curacao. She also had carrier pigeons and sent back messages. Chin, the alchemist in Port Royal, was keeping

Bill informed about matters on St. Eustatius through his connections with the Chinese community on the island.

That night in the Cathedral, the plans to take St. Eustatius and Providence were set down. Bill heard the echo of footsteps and men's voices coming into the cavern.

Looking carefully at Morgan, he said, "Are you ready to brief these captains? This is your chance, Morgan, to show some leadership."

As he looked up, he saw John Davis and Francois l'Olonnais silhouetted under the torch carried by Mansvelt as they entered the subterranean chamber where Morgan and Bill sat. Behind them followed the Roach, Johnson the Terrible, Young Calico Jack, Jacquotte Delahaye, Captain Freeman, and Black Bart. Lieutenant Brossard followed behind Jacquotte.

While the captains gathered around the table, Morgan spread Bill's Spanish maps and detailed plans of fortifications under the dim light of the candles that rested in the chandeliers above the table.

"The Dutch island called the Golden Rock, gentlemen. The island of St. Eustatius, as you know, is sometimes called Statia. It sits here"—Morgan pointed to a place on the map—"among the Leeward Islands at 17° 30' north. It's owned by the Dutch West India Company and is one of the Netherlands's most important free-trading ports in the Caribbean. Chiefly, they sell arms and ammunition to anyone willing to pay the price. These munitions come from their factories in Holland. Crippling their port and capturing the guns and ammunition would, of course, be the reason for attacking this particular Dutch settlement and one that Governor Modyford could only applaud. There are no real fortified defenses onshore. Dutch warships in the harbor would be their only possible protection against any attack."

Bill drifted back into the shadows of the cavern, listening to every word that Morgan spoke. Amazingly, Morgan no longer appeared drunk. Every word was crisp and clean, each action choreographed to the audience. Morgan, if nothing else, was a great leader of men.

"Davis, Jacquotte, Johnson, Freeman, and I will take a small fleet of ten or twelve ships and seven hundred men against this target," Morgan stated. "Modyford will provide the legal order of marque. And, Jacquotte, there is also a large settlement of Chinese on this island. The Chinese supply the labor for the hazardous work of loading and unloading the munitions. There are young Chinese girls, Jacquotte. You do still fancy young Chinese girls, don't you?" Morgan whispered secretively into Jacquotte's ear.

She squealed, and her eyes lit up. "Chinese girls, you say? All the better." And she glanced knowingly in Brossard's direction.

John Davis or Robert Searle, whichever name he might be called, remained silent. No one really knew much about him, where he actually came from, what his true family name might have been, or why he had ended up as a privateer in the West Indies. He was undoubtedly an English gentleman. His attire, the way he carried himself, and the way he spoke all came from an education and upbringing that could have only come from an English upper-class environment. But he was not much in the way of a sea captain and actually knew very little about navigation or ships. He had, however, a commanding presence and a bold daring about him that men seemed to follow. John Davis, like Morgan, was a leader of men, and they seemed to follow him unquestionably.

"John," Morgan said, "after we capture St. Eustatius, we'll divide our squadron of ships into two divisions. I'll keep one division at St. Eustatius to sack the city of gold and whatever ransom can be obtained. The other division you will lead, John. Load all the munitions you can carry on these ships and sail to where Captain Mansvelt waits.

"Mansvelt and Bart, I have something special for both you, and Captain l'Olonnais and Captain Braziliano." Morgan smiled. "The Spanish Isla de Providence, which is sometimes called Santa Catalina, that lies about 140 miles off the coast of Nicaragua. The Spanish took this island from the English in 1641. Providence is the English name. And there are still a few English Puritan settlers running small plantations there that would welcome your arrival. The only fortifications are on a small island, which guards the sea passage into the open harbor. A bridge connects the island to the fortress. Here are the plans of the Spanish fort and diagrams of the placement of the cannons. Walker's Gypsy friends have been in and around this island group of San Andres and Santa Catalina for the last two months, and they confirm that fortifications and the cannon placement are as we see before us.

"Our friends also tell me that less than two hundred Spanish soldiers are stationed there. Captain Walker will take sixty of his trained raiders and land them on the west side of Santa Catalina. During the night, he will take his men across the island by land and attack the fort before dawn. These raiders will silence the guns that guard the narrow passageway that leads into the harbor. Mansvelt, you and Francois attack Providence at dawn.

"John Davis, load your ships with as much captured munitions from St. Eustatius as you can carry and secretly sail for Providence. Don't waste a moment. We will need those munitions to hold the island against counterattack from the Spanish. I'll take the remainder of our squadron and make port in Jamaica to both reassure the governor, giving him a Dutch defeat that he can report to England and disguise our true purpose. Then I'll sail for Providence as well, bringing as many Captains of the Coast and their ships as I can manage."

Secret Code

15 February 1665, 10:00 a.m.
Captain's cabin, the Commencement

Sir Harold had explained to William while he was in England the importance of information and how to relay information in a form that, if intercepted, did not betray either the sender or who was receiving the document. His father used similar methods, and because both his father and Dobbs had provided Bill with their contacts in the West Indies and sent him messages, a method had to be devised to assure that the information was secure and the contacts protected.

"It's simple, my boy," explained Sir Harold. "A code, a different language, if you will. A little trick passed down from Sir William Cecil and Sir Francis Walsingham under Queen Elizabeth, who reportedly used these techniques extensively for an intelligence network she commissioned called Rainbow. Sir Isaac Newton picked the idea up recently and wrote a paper on the subject. Did you know that Julius Caesar used a cipher called the perfect square to deliver his messages to his commanders? Numbers for letters, letters transposed into symbols, the alphabet just arranged differently by the sender, and then rearranged when it's received. It's been done for centuries. But the problem is if the code is too devious, it becomes unusable for many people, just too damn complicated. However, if it's too easy, it can eventually be undone by your opponent. Something simple and not too devious is what's called for in this case.

"We'll use a code word to encrypt our messages. Your father's informants and mine are already referred to not by their true names but by a code name. Therefore, what I suggest is that we use that code name to devise a unique cipher for each informant your father and I have. Using this method will assure that if one spy is captured or one message decoded, it will not compromise the next.

"Let's say we have an agent called Othello. Now the code word for the cipher is therefore Othello. Arrange the alphabet as usual *A* to *Z*."

> A B C D E F G H I J K L M N O P Q R S T U V W X Y Z

"Under that, start with the code word *Othello*. Don't duplicate letters, so it reads *Othel*, and you have something that looks like this."

> A B C D E F G H I J K L M N O P Q R S T U V W X Y Z
> O T H E L A B C D F G I J K M N P Q R S U V W X Y Z

"If you receive a message from Othello that reads 'RCDN OQDVDKB COVOKO,' reverse the code to read 'Ship arriving Havana,'" explained Sir Harold.

"Now, you'll have to memorize the code names of the agents and the methods we have worked out to contact them. Nothing can be written in this matter. Each agent that your father and I reveal to you also has a network of agents, which you will not know about. It's for their safety and yours."

Bill sat in his cabin aboard the *Commencement* writing a detailed letter that he then put into code to Sir Harold. He explained everything. He began the letter with the chance encounter on the island of Curacao with Mansvelt and Morgan and their voyage back to Jamaica, where he enlisted their support in forming the clandestine navy that Sir Harold instructed him to create. He described the meeting of the captains in the Cathedral under Port Royal. He told Sir Harold about the sacking of Villa de Mosa, Rio Garta, Truxillo, and the city of Granda. And he described Modyford's response and the meeting that he was compelled to attend with Morgan and the governor at King's House. He described the plans for attacking the Dutch island of St. Eustatius and capturing the munitions held there. He further outlined the plan of also capturing the island of

Providence and its strategic importance as a staging point and how the munitions captured from St. Eustatius would support further privateer raids along the Spanish Main. Bill ended the lengthy letter with a cautionary comment:

> An unusual force of arms has now been created. And I must mention that this undertaking has been done at your request alone. I must caution you, these men that are now gathered together are motivated by greed alone. They are all self-reliant souls and resourceful. They are resourceful beyond anything that you can envision. Most confess no allegiance to any country. They are now held together by the strength of one man. That man is Mansvelt. Morgan? Morgan, with all his faults aside, is a natural-born leader of ruthless men, and if anything were to happen to Mansvelt, Morgan could definitely slip into his place just as you wished. My fear, Sir Harold, is that you have created something that cannot be undone. Your fondness of the playwright Shakespeare reminds me of one quote from his play *Julius Caesar*, a quote that I think you are surely familiar with, act 3, scene 1: "Cry 'Havoc!' and let slip the dogs of war." As you know, Mark Antony's "dogs of war" were soldiers unleashed by their commander's orders to wreak general havoc, including rape, pillage, and plunder. And that,

Sir Harold, is what these men will do. My fear is that now that you have unleashed your dogs, there will be no calling them back.

Lilly

22 March 1665, 6:00 p.m.
Montego Bay, Jamaica

The waves graciously washed over her slim brown thighs, and the sand gathered in a warming comfortable mass between her long, hard, adolescent, legs; each wave came across her in a refreshing relief. The white sand gathered wistfully in shallow wet piles, spreading around her firm, hard hips and pursuing an unquestionable course, washing over her silky-smooth thighs, where it settled between her legs. She lay on the beach, naked and alone in her thoughts. Her tall, slender body was warmed by the sun, and dreams of youthful fantasies filled her mind, fantasies that were yet but hopefully to be experienced. As she stood and brushed the sand from her body, she closely studied herself. She breathed deeply, reflectively, and thought, *Is it a nice body?* She was very tall, brown, and slim with a young girl's eagerness of reaching seventeen years old and had the youthful uncertainty of how her body might appear to others. She sometimes thought that her long muscular legs and arms were ungainly and that her small firm breasts weren't large enough to please a man. And that her large, prominent brown nipples that were so very responsive to her touch were too large. And she felt that the crop of thick, matted, moist black hair that was just starting to spread between her legs was decadent, possibly even sinful. "I guess it's a nice body. But am I beautiful?" she asked herself. Her amber catlike eyes with long black lashes sparkled under heavy dark brows and thick, long, wet light brown hair hung down her back. "I guess it's a nice body?" she questioned again, unsure and undecided.

She had known Captain William Walker since she had come to her new home in Jamaica with her father. Edward, her father, had often invited the young captain to King's House for dinner and meetings. From the first time that she had seen him standing rigid in his blue-and-white navy uniform and powdered wig before her father in the foyer of the governor's house, he was her fantasy. On his return visits, he brought her treasures from his ventures: gold necklaces with bright red rubies, jeweled turquoise rings, and flowers; he always brought her flowers. And he would tell her stories. After that first meeting, her fantasies started. She would silently wait for him in her fitful sleepless nights, hoping that he would secretly come into her room and make love to her. But he never came. Now she waited for him on the beach of Montego Bay and wondered if this man would find her desirable. Would he love her? Would he make love to her as she had dreamed? Rachel had assured her this very morning that he would come. She had said that he would come to her, and he would love her if that was what she wished. And Rachel had explained to her what to do if she wanted this man.

Bill did come to her. He had sailed from Port Royal aboard his ship, the *Commencement*, bound for Providence, but making a short detour to Montego Bay so that he could be with her. He had to see her. And so he crossed the sea to where she was. He came to her out of his own restless yearning.

The *Commencement* lay in the harbor, her sails luffing in the wind as her anchor came to rest in the soft sand. Bill swam to where he had seen Lilly lying on the beach. With her image in sight, he swam toward shore, toward her. She was standing unclothed at the water's edge some yards away as he swam out of the turquoise underbelly of the white-capped surf that washed the beach.

The *Commencement* stood anchored in Montego Bay while Bill and Lilly made love in the tropical paradise of the island's retreat. In the dark night they first embraced was rested on a low mattress of silklike palm fibers that were wrapped tightly in cover of loose white linen fabric. The rickety timber floor underneath squeaked in submissive response to the lovers above. Jagua had given Bill a large leather pouch of moist green coca leaves, which he shared with Elizabeth. Her dilated amber eyes sparkled lustfully, and her body glistened with moist perspiration as she chewed the leaves, drank wine, and they found each other.

During the day Rachel, Elizabeth's escort, and one black woman from the island catered the young couple's needs as they ran and played like children along the beach, swimming joyfully into the pounding blue crescent waves that washed ashore. At the end of the day they laid on the warm sand together, helplessly in each other's arms. Both the wine and the exotic flavor of the coca leaves accentuated their passion, and they made love both day and night until all was lost in heavenly satisfaction, and greedily they held each other in limp tangled arms and legs, each hoping that the next day they spent together would be like the last and each day after would be like the first time that they had made love.

Within those few days that they had together, Bill thought that he loved Elizabeth. Her young sixteen-year-old body never seemed to tire of his desire for her. Unlike Cat or the other women in his life, Elizabeth could be a bride that would be accepted in London circles and the mother of children that also would be recognized and accepted by his father and British society. Her body and her spirit taunted him as the days passed, embracing each other in ecstasy, each day better and more gratifying than the last. Her touch and her kiss never became old, and he longed for both as he lay beside her.

The days spent with Elizabeth collided with Bill's duties, but finally there came a time that he had to leave her. Catlina, his father, Sir Harold, and now Morgan all pulled against every fiber of his being as he kissed her.

"Lilly," Bill declared as he pulled from her grasp, "Mary Elizabeth Morgan, I love you, my dear child!" He looked into her bright amber eyes. "But I must leave on the tide. My ship awaits, and I have a duty to carry out."

"William!" she cried in a light, throaty, childlike voice as tears came to her eyes. "My love," she pleaded desperately, holding him close to her, "don't leave me. Not now. Don't leave me, ever!" She started to cry. Her wet tears fell onto Bill's chest as he held her in his arms.

Pushing her away, he softly spoke, "I must go, my love."

Reluctantly, Bill dressed and, leaving Elizabeth, made his way to the beach as she followed. A longboat waited on the shore that would take him back to the ship anchored in the harbor. Elizabeth, in only a light white cotton dress, walked into the water behind him. The wet dress clung to her supple young body, and she stood at the shore waving good-bye as the small boat, pulled by four oarsmen, made its way across the turquoise blue waters toward the *Commencement*. She watched as the ship's sails unfolded from the white spars.

As William and the longboat were taken aboard the ship, Lilly heard Big Daniel's voice shout, "Weigh anchor, lads! Look lively now!" And she whispered to herself, "Godspeed, my love."

William came alongside the ship as the anchor was being pulled from the bottom of the sea. Looking high into the rigging, he watched the first sails dropping and heard the snap of the canvas catching the wind. He heard the sound of the capstan's heavy clicks as it turned, and he heard the men pushing the spoke of the capstan singing a familiar sea chantey. Captain William Walker smiled as he looked around his ship.

"This is the life," he said to himself. "Nothing else could possibly be better."

And the thought of Elizabeth faded in his memory.

"Orders?" Daniel asked as Bill came onto the quarterdeck.

"We rendezvous with Mansvelt and the other captains off Monkey Key."

"And then where?" Big Daniel questioned. "The crew wants to know."

"It be Providence, Dannie, and six months of raiding and plunder that the likes of these men have never seen before. More gold than any can imagine."

Raid on Providence

18 June 1665, 3:00 a.m.
la Cortadua Castle, Isla de Providence

The Spanish captain held Francisca in his arms as he watched the murderous band of pirates spread through the castle's compound slaughtering his soldiers. Explosions erupted around him, and clouds of smoke hung in the hot, humid air, blocking his sight. The young man, bewildered and not knowing what to do in the midst of the battle's confusion, did the only thing that he could think of at the moment. He clutched the frail, long-haired, brown Gypsy girl closer to his side, his saber drawn. He thought to himself, *Alone I will defend her against these brigands, these pirates that have invaded my castle. I will defend her to my death!*

Out of the smoke of the gunfire and the explosions, a figure materialized before him. "Yield, my young lad!" the voice shouted.

Before he knew what was happening, Francisca was pulled from his arms, and he felt the cold sharp edge of steel resting across his throat. "Surrender, and on my word, you and your men will not be killed," the voice commanded. Bill had always found that leniency regarding prisoners and captives was the best policy. A man knowing that he would either die or be tortured would fight to the death. But even when the foe greatly outnumbered Bill's privateers, they would likely surrender rather than fight if they knew that freedom was at hand. "Yield." Bill pulled Francisca into his arms, the young captain helpless.

With a cutlass blade against his neck, the young Spanish captain saw the smile on the Gypsy woman's face as she pulled away from him and looked into the cold eyes of his adversary—Bloody Bill Walker.

"I yield," he stated.

Three days before, Mansvelt's fleet of nine ships and two hundred men approached the island of Providence from the northwest where he set anchor some three leagues offshore well outside the barrier reef that surrounded most of the island. Twenty men were lowered onto two longboats and, led by Jagua and two of her sisters, traveled by an unusual passage through the reefs. Cat had been waiting for William as he landed with his small force onshore at a place called Playa de los Naranjos on the maps that Bill had. Silently, so as not to attract any attention from the armed settlement just southeast at Playa Grande, Bill unloaded his men, weapons, and fifteen casks of rum from the longboats. To the east of their landing point, cradled inside an L-shaped chain of small volcanic mountains that ran from the west of Playa de los Naranjos and ended at an easterly point just behind Playa Grande, were open fields that had been planted in sugarcane. To the west these mountains ran right up against the sea, ending in high cliffs. A freshwater river tumbled down from the hilltops and spilled into the shallow sea basin below the cliffs. It was this freshwater from the river that had carved out the narrow, twisted passageway through the coral reef that Jagua had found. Around the tip of the island on the windward side was Aguada Grande, where the governor's house was located. Cerro de la Hermosa was the name of the much higher volcanic mountain chain that ran down the center of the island.

Cat guided Bill and his men inland along a brackish river through a tangled mangrove swamp that ran between the central mountains to the west and the L-shaped smaller mountain chain to the east. There were no boats. The water level was too low. The men slugged through the swamp-like terrain hauling the heavy rum barrels and armaments that they had unloaded at the bay on tired, aching shoulders.

For two days they walked through this hell; each step seemed to be more difficult than the last. On the third night, they finally came to the harbor and saw the lights of La Cartadura on Isla Chica. And they saw the bridge that connected Providence to the island where the fortress of El Castille sat guarding the harbor. Santa Teresa Castille was the Spanish fort that guarded the passageway into the harbor of Providence.

As in Cuba and elsewhere, they played out the all-too-familiar deception. Cat's tribe of Gypsies would land at a port months before Bill's planned attack. They gathered information and sent carrier pigeons with the information back to Bill at the secluded island where the pigeon nests were kept. The Gypsy tribe of dancers, musicians, and animal trainers would entertain the Spanish soldiers, and after weeks, the Gypsies would seem to pose no threat, and the Spanish welcomed them into their cities, forts, and castles.

This time, however, it was not Cat but Francisca, who was now fifteen years old, who had endeared herself to the Spanish captain that commanded the castle. The captain, with encouragement from Francisca, had planned a celebration, timed to Bill's arrival, for the soldiers at his post. Brightly painted Gypsy wagons pulled by black horses with bells ringing rolled through the open gates into the compound. Young girls with silky smooth brown skin and raven-black hair with wide, flashing dark eyes stepped down from the colorful wagons and into the arms of the Spanish soldiers that stood in amazement, Francisca leading the way.

Once inside, Bill and twenty of his men all dressed in Gypsy clothing dropped from the wagons and unloaded the barrels of rum that Bill had brought with him. Bright fires were lit in the courtyard, and the Spanish men in the camp saw no reason why they should not enjoy this celebration.

The music began, and in the firelight, William and his men, weapons hidden, spread through the castle. It was a small castle built on the side of the bay overlooking the harbor. But it presented a stark display of power with heavy cannons sprouting from every portal. Unlike many fortifications built of mud bricks, this one was built from stone with large turrets and bunkers. The cannons were placed to cover an attack from any side. Santa Teresa had once been well armed and fortified, but like many Spanish settlements, the troops were undertrained, most being conscripts, and they were commanded by less-than-skillful officers.

The garrison was not the mighty fortification it had once been. Lack of suitable troops, indifference, corruption, and apathy had all taken their toll. El Castille should have been manned by 140 regular troops. But few commands in the Spanish Indies were ever up to strength. There were only ninety soldiers stationed on the entire island, twenty of whom were either too sick or too old to bear arms. Most of the officers had been sent to the island as exiles. Four years at Santa Catalina was a common punishment for delinquent junior officers on the mainland. Many of the Spanish women on the island were also exiles from cities like Portobello, Cartagena, and Panama, where their scandalous behavior warranted their removal.

First setting fire to the munitions bunker and then disabling the cannons by crippling the gun carriages with explosives so that the weapons could not be aimed, the twenty highly skilled warriors captured the few Spanish soldiers at the fort. As daylight hit the east wall of the castle, Mansvelt sailed into the harbor, his cannons roaring, and unloaded the remainder of the privateer troops.

The next day, the twenty-seven cannon carriages that sat inside Santa Teresa castle were easily repaired, and the loss of the munitions was of little consequence. Now the great guns stood as a deterrent to any future invasion. Bill now controlled the island. Captain John Davis, after capturing St. Eustatius with Morgan, loaded his three ships with the Dutch munitions and made his way into the harbor the following day. With this shipment of gunpowder and the additional men and ships that Davis brought, the Captains of the Coast now controlled this part of the fabulous Spanish Main. More privateer ships followed Davis during the next few weeks. Now with twenty ships and over a thousand men, the English privateers were masters of these waters and could attack any Spanish fortification on the mainland they chose, always knowing that they could come back to Providence to unload their booty and resupply their ships.

A month later the grand ballroom of Santa Teresa castle was filled with one hundred or more drunken privateers. Dasha, Cat, and Francisca, skirts lifted high, danced. The captive Spanish officers and their men also sat at the tables in the ballroom, drinking alongside their adversaries. The Spanish harlots that had been deported to this godforsaken island reveled in release and bedded any willing sailor, asking that he just take her somewhere else. All were enjoying themselves while Bill, Davis, and l'Olonnais sat at a long table at the center of the room with Catlina and Francisca. The Roach and Black

Bart were around somewhere, probably with Mansvelt, arguing over plunder.

"Tell me, John, what happened at St. Eustatius?" Bill asked Davis.

The men and women around the table sat silent as John Davis told his story.

"After leaving Port Royal, Morgan lost two vessels, lost them in a storm only two days out," Captain Davis explained. "So Morgan was left with only 326 men for the assault. The Spanish maps that you provided showed the exact location and sailing instructions into a hidden landing place on the south side of the island. Coming off the beach where the ships anchored, we followed a narrow path that led up a mountain. The path was so narrow that only two men at a time could walk up the hill. At the top stood the Dutch fortification armed with 450 Dutchmen and cannons. Colonel Morgan, I'm sorry to say, was overcome by heat as he led his men up the mountainside. He died later on the hillside. As we came off the hill, we encountered troops settled in tents around the fort. The enemy fired only one volley of musket fire, and when we returned fire, they retreated into the fort. Captain Morgan sent an envoy demanding surrender. He promised that those in the fort and the city would be spared if the Dutch surrendered, but if they did not, he promised that every man, woman, and child would be put to the sword. The Dutch captain surrendered.

"Meanwhile, Jacquotte took seventy men and crossed over to the island of Saba, only four leagues distant, and secured its surrender under the same terms as St. Eustatius. But without Mansvelt, Morgan was unable to hold the Captains of the Coast or their crew together after the battle, and they fought over the division of the spoils. Most of the captains demanded that a settlement be made on the spot and each to go their way. Divided out was something like £100,000 of silver and gold, nine hundred slaves, livestock, and bales of cotton. The guns and munitions that we needed here were loaded aboard my ships as we had planned."

A few days later, Mansvelt left Providence with most of the fleet to plunder Spanish settlements. Their departure left only a few men and ships under Bill's command to hold the island. Mansvelt sailed with the prisoners from Providence for Central America. After dropping the Spanish prisoners ashore on the mainland, Mansvelt boldly sailed up the San Juan River to sack the city of Granada, the Spanish capital of Nicaragua. From Granada, his ships turned south into Costa Rico. Everywhere he landed, a path of destruction followed. Mansvelt burned plantations and destroyed churches, shot cattle and livestock indiscriminately, burned people alive, cut down fruit trees, and in general, destroyed everything in his path as his men crossed the countryside. Rumors of his terror spread, and town after town capitulated under the threat of their wrath.

While Mansvelt plundered the Spanish Main, Bill held the fragile stronghold of Providence, the British key to the Spanish Main, in the name of Morgan. Morgan was supposed to lead the next fleet. Where was Morgan? All the other Captains of the Coast had gathered under Morgan's flag at Providence, assuming that Morgan was to be in command of a second fleet. But without Morgan, most had struck out on their own, attacking Spanish settlements wherever they might be found. It was what Bill had always feared; how do you hold men together once they had a few doubloons in their pockets? How do you keep them fighting? Mansvelt either already knew the secret or accidentally discovered the secret. Keep the men engaged in long campaigns, hitting town after town in quick succession. No rest, don't divide the spoils, don't go back to port, keep the men fighting. That was the secret.

Bill spent his time on Providence making love to Cat and trying to plan and direct attacks and organizing shipments of plunder back to Jamaica. Privateer ships came into the harbor, unloaded their captured goods, and then were resupplied then sent back out to raid more Spanish towns. Walker organized convoys of four to five lightly armed merchant ships that left from Providence, slipping around the Spanish blockade every two to three weeks, bound for Port Royal, their holes loaded with captured treasures. The ships then returned to Providence, bringing back supplies.

During these months, Bill sent several more coded messages back to Sir Harold, informing him of every detail. He thought of Lilly as he held Cat in his arms. He longed to be back with her.

Río de la Muerte

26 November 1665, 3:00 a.m.
el Morro Fortress, Habana de Cuba

The sound of cannon fire from the Twelve Apostles announced nine o'clock. Martin watched as the gates to San Cristobal de la Habana were being closed. The walled city now rested comfortably in the night guarded by a twelve-piece heavy-artillery battery inside Castillo de los Tres Reyes Magos del Morro. A heavy chain was being stretched across the mouth of the harbor from the base of the castle to the smaller fort at La Punta that sat on the other side of the bay. The lighthouse on a rocky promontory point that jutted into the sea under El Morro Castle flashed its white beacon into the night.

The massive fortress was named after the biblical Magi and shared the same name as the fortresses that had been built in San Juan de Puerto and Santiago de Cuba. Perched on the rocky promontory on the opposite side of the harbor from the city of Havana, it dominated the port entrance. Construction had begun in 1589, and Martin finally finished the construction by adding the artillery battery, which came to be known as the Twelve Apostles. Every evening at nine o'clock, the massive cannons fired a shot, announcing the closing of the gates and the harbor.

The loss of his eye still bothered him as he rubbed the black leather oval that covered the hollow cavity where his eye once rested. Bringing a moist handkerchief to the corner of the black patch, he dabbed a drop of blood-tinged tear before it could trickle down his face. Martin remembered the night vividly. Catlina was fighting, struggling on the bed where he thought he had her captive. In one single unguarded moment, she was on him like a falcon. Before he knew what was happening, her long red-lacquered talons tore at his face, and she plucked his eye from his head like a grape. Had it not been for Walker, he would have killed her that night. Or maybe they might have killed each other.

Martin stood on the northern ramparts of El Morro, looking out over the black sea that was only momentarily lit by the blinking beacon of the lighthouse as it rotated around a half-circle axis. Since that fateful night with Catlina and Bloody Bill's raid on his residence in the town, Martin had not returned to the city or his home. He had all his possessions moved from the house to the castle, where he now lived in seclusion. A squad of heavily armed soldiers guarded his quarters inside the castle twenty-four hours a day. *What happened?* he thought. *I let my guard down. I let that woman seduce me. Well, not again. Never again.*

"I must focus all my efforts on but one thing: Coriancha." He said the name softly under a deep exhaled breath. "Coriancha." The admiral's heavy hand fell across Castillo de los Tres Reyes Magos del Morro like a fist. There were no more parties. The fortress was virtually sealed, and the troops had been on alert, battle ready, for months. The only time Martin left his quarters inside the castle was for his nightly visits to the prison cells in the dungeon below the castle or to his ship.

And Walker, Walker now jeopardizes my quest for Coriancha. Now that the English hold the island of Providence, they control the Spanish Main. Their raids of shipping and attacks on the mainland were once only irritating, trivial. But now these brigands attack in force under one command. They're taking every port, raiding every settlement, burning crops, raping and pillaging, torturing, and murdering whole cities. My position as admiral in these waters is being threatened. I must combat these pirates or at least hold them at bay until I can find the Golden City.

His thoughts were interrupted by a heavy knock on the door.

An orderly led Captain Jose Eduardo Santos Tavares Melo Silva into the dark room that evening and presented him to the Spanish admiral.

"Please bring Eduardo a glass," he ordered.

The young soldier obeyed and went to the cabinet under the window where he knew the bottles of whiskey were kept. He poured a glass for both the admiral and his guest and moved across the room, handing each man his drink. Then closing the door of the admiral's quarters, he left the room.

"Welcome back, Silva. Did you find the river?" exclaimed the admiral. Silva watched as the man nervously twisted the silver ring on his left hand around his finger, caressing the strange raised emblem of crossed swords over a crucifix as his cold black eyes stared at Silva.

Captain Silva slumped into a chair with his head bent.

"Yes, Your Excellency," Silva began. "With the old man as a guide, we sailed from Curacao to South America. We found the river. Río de la Muerte it is called. And after traveling up the river, we found the lagoon. Once inside the lagoon, I anchored, and I built barges. We dredged the river bottom for any of the treasure that the old sailor said he and the girl had taken down river from the city and lost in the lagoon. Only a few pieces were found."

Interrupting Silva's narrative, Martin asked, "You say that you found part of the treasure?"

"Yes, as I said, a few pieces."

"But if you found something, it proves that the old man's story to be true. Don't you see?"

"Oh, the story is true enough, Your Excellency. It is true enough. The pieces that we found when we dredged the lagoon were not Inca or Aztec. Or even Mayan. They were golden objects with Coptic Greek writing on them."

"How do you know this?" Martin asked.

"A man aboard my ship identified the writing on the golden stones."

"Where are these few pieces of gold now?"

"Safe, Your Excellency, safe somewhere outside your reach."

"Very well, Silva, you say that you left from Curacao? Does anyone on Curacao know about where you planned to sail or what your venture was?"

"Possibly," Silva responded. "The owner of the tavern where I found the old Portuguese sailor might have guessed what we were up to."

"Who is this tavern owner?"

"A man named Boot. He runs the Dode Paard Tavern in Willemstad."

Changing the subject, Martin questioned the man further. "So you found the mouth of the river and the lagoon? And you found some of the treasure that the man said he lost during the trip downriver with the girl? What did you do then?"

"Yes, we found some of the treasure, and the old sailor said that he could guide me to the hidden city using his maps. I sent fifty heavily armed men with the old man in five barges down the river into the jungle. Each barge was armed with swivel cannons and loaded with supplies, powder, and ammunition."

He held up his glass, and Martin poured out another eight ounces of whiskey that he gulped down, and he lifted his hand for more.

"Your Excellency, I sat for a year, a year in this lagoon, waiting. The river that I had sent the barges into led for miles and miles through the jungle," he said as he greedily drank another glass. "Messages came back. First one man and then, months later, another man made their way back to the ship. Both were delirious with fever. The dying men told stories of horrors along the river, large snakes that could swallow a whole man, plants that ate the skin off your bones, insects that burrowed underneath the skin and eventually drove a man crazy as they ate their way into the brain, and carnivorous fish that infested the river that could strip a man to the bone in seconds. And crocodiles. Crocodiles that would attack the floating barges at night, carrying sleeping men on deck into the black waters. The dying men that came back to the ship said the natives along the river were cannibals that killed with poison darts and arrows. They said shrunken human heads hung from trees along the riverbank.

"I waited a year, Your Excellency, in that godforsaken lagoon while men on board my ship died from fever. After a year, a single barge returned with only two crewmen that mumbled incoherently about a golden city," Eduardo explained, now crying and gulping down more whiskey. "The old sailor must have died with the rest. At any rate, he didn't come back. After the single barge returned during the night, natives attacked the ship. Before I knew what was happening, they had killed most of my crew. I barely escaped."

Silva slumped further into the chair as Martin handed him another glass of whiskey, which he also gulped down in a single throw.

"I'll have nothing more to do with any of this. The place is cursed. I'm rid of it all," Silva said as Martin poured more whiskey into his glass.

"And I'm rid of you too!" Eduardo exclaimed as he finished off the last glass that Martin had poured. "I'm rid of your folly! I've lost most of my crew, and I have nothing to show for it. I want one hundred thousand pesos now!" Eduardo stood and pulled a gun from under his vest. The man's hand shook, but the gun was pointed at Martin, and at that range, he couldn't miss.

"Very well then, I'll give you what you want, Eduardo. But you must give me what I want.

The admiral carefully moved from behind his desk and walked to a large sea chest that sat along one wall. He inserted a key into a bronze lock. Opening the chest, the admiral pulled out several leather bags of doubloons and, untying the tops of the bags, spilled out the gold on the floor in front of Eduardo.

"Here, take what you want," the admiral said. "There's no need for guns, my friend. But what I want is the location of the river and the maps, Eduardo. Where are the old sailor's drawings? Where is Río de la Muerte? Where are the gold objects that you found?"

The mercenary captain pulled a handful of papers from the pocket of his coat and threw them at the admiral.

"Find it yourself, you bastard. I'll have nothing more to do with that godforsaken place."

Eduardo tried to gather the scattered gold coins from the floor.

A single gunshot was heard outside the admiral's door by the guards. As they rushed into the room, the men saw Martin holding a small smoking pistol in his left hand. They quickly grabbed the wounded man lying on the floor. Then kneeling down and grabbing Silva's face in his hand, Martin looked directly into the man's eyes.

"You'll tell me everything, my friend. Do you understand? Everything. And I'll enjoy our discussions. You know, it's been a long time since I have used my skills. I'll enjoy this."

"Take him to the castle's dungeon!" Martin shouted as he stroked the silver ring on his finger.

After the guards had taken Silva from the room, Martin gathered the drawings that Silva had given him. He sat quietly for the next few hours, studying faded drawings, trying to arrange the pages in some kind of order that might tell him the story of the old man's journey down the river. What new information did these drawings add to what Martin already knew?

Sitting in the dark room Martin remembered the events that had brought him to this point. He had left the church after finding what he believed to be conclusive evidence that the city existed. Coriancha, the Temple of the Sun, actually existed! After leaving the church, he gained his appointment to the Caribbean through bribes. Before leaving Spain for the Caribe, another curious event unfolded; another piece of the puzzle fell into place. Martin was ordered to a secret meeting with the Director General of the La Casa y Audiencia de Indies in Seville where he had been shown a number of sealed documents. One of these documents was a strange order written in Latin that he read fluently and signed by Pope Paul III in 1542 called the Quinta Directiva. This holy edict was so secret that even knowledge that it existed could mean death.

During this meeting, Martin was only allowed to see the document, not take it with him. It sternly ordered that any evidence of European existence in the West Indies that might have come before 1492 and the discovery of the New World by Christopher Columbus were to be destroyed. *"What was the real meaning and intent behind this directive?"* he asked himself.

The Fifth Directive said nothing about the possibility of white tribes in the New World. But Martin had found records both in the monasteries of Spain and at Santiago Abbey that these tribes existed. Or was there mention of cities of gold? But again, Martin had found records written by men who had actually seen this city. And there was no mention of the possibility of ancient religious artifacts that supposedly came from the time of Moses and Solomon. But now, Silva claims to have found Greek inscriptions on golden objects that he found at the mouth of the river. There was no mention of a white god, Viracocha, and a white tribe that the natives call the Chachapoya. But the natives Martin had captured and tortured confessed not only knowledge of this god but some had actually seen the Chachapoys.

"And now I have these drawings, pictures of the trail that leads to the city. And finally," he said, holding one of the drawings in his hand, "I have a picture of the city itself. The evidence is there. The city actually existed.

"Why would the church want all evidence of white tribes in the New World eradicated? Could it be because stories of the white god Viracocha and the Chachapoys are linked to Coriancha? Is the church trying to hide the evidence until one of its lazy friars happens to stumble across the location?"

Martin knew that in this day and age, religion was politics. Every Roman Catholic monarchy had to be sanctified by the pope in order to gain the title of either king or queen. Royal marriages also had to have the pope's blessing. England had been the first to break away from the church in Rome. Henry had simply created the Church of England and named himself as the holy spiritual leader of this new Protestant Christian religion. England's King James even had the audacity to translate the Latin Bible into English. Now more and more Christian religions were being formed. Politics was religion. The taxes that the Church of Rome once collected on church properties were now rapidly diminishing. The once infallible power of Rome was rapidly slipping.

"Silva will reveal everything that he knows," Martin said to himself.

"Orderly!" Martin screamed as he pushed aside a stack of records on his desk, clearing a space. "Orderly!"

The bright, brown-faced young man with a penciled line of a black mustache opened the doors to Martin's study and entered the room for the third time that evening.

"Your Excellency," the young man said.

"Where is the *Anglice* galleons?"

"As you know, they will be here soon. A week maybe?"

"How many warships accompany this convoy?"

"As always, five," the young man responded.

"Close all the ports. Nothing goes in and nothing goes out without my written approval. Bring me all the maps that we have of the island of Providence."

Smoke and Oakum

*19 December 1665, 12:00 a.m.
Position unknown, Caribbean Sea*

It was still raining. For the second time in the last half hour, Bill studied the storm glass. It hadn't changed. Bright blue crystals still floated in the milky fluid inside the chamber. But Bill noted, still examining the chamber, that there were not a lot of crystals. He had certainly seen more in these latitudes. So the rains might not be the first signs of what he feared—a tropical storm. The rain and the wind that hit his face as he left his cabin on the way to the quarterdeck were warm. There was no need for an oilskin cloak. It was almost noon. Looking across the choppy, white-capped green sea, what could be seen of the horizon was a deep purple. There was no sun. It would be another day that the ship could not fix her position.

It had been five days now that they had sailed in rain and storms, never once sighting the sun or stars to acquire latitude. Bill had ordered a course of ten points off twenty degrees west by northeast. But the storm had made the currents and the winds unpredictable. So a true course to make good was anybody's guess. But guesses like this were so often what made the difference between good captains and bad captains. Much, as Bill knew, was just luck.

Will I be a lucky captain this time around? Bill asked himself. Eight bells sounded. The bell signaled noon. Through the rain, muffled reassuring cries from the lookouts came from around the ship: "Starboard bow, all's well! Starboard gangway, all's well!" It was followed by "All's well!" from across the rest of the ship. "Twenty inches in the well," another man reported.

"Man the pumps!" the boatswain replied. "Heave the log!" And a sailor threw a line into the water. Attached at one end of this line was a wooden plank shaped like a piece of pie that was weighted with lead along the base of the triangular arc. It tried to float point up in the water, but the waves whipped it around until it finally plunged below the surface. Knots were tied every 47.33 feet along the line, and a sailor counted out the knots as the line tore through his fingers. A twenty-eight-second glass turned, and as the last grain of sand ran out, the man called, "Fifteen knots, sir."

Another sailor cried out, "Wind on the port quarter, heading west by northeast!"

"Mr. Cribb, drop the topgallants. If this wind picks up any more, we'll lose them."

"Aye, Cap'n," Cribb replied then ordered the boatswain to pipe quarters. At the sound of the boatswain's pipe, men ran on deck. "Slack the starboard and larboard lifts. Lower the topgallants! Easy now, lads, mind the wind leeward."

As the sails dropped, the ship rolled to the starboard side for just a moment until the helmsman could correct the position of the ship, bringing the helm around to catch the wind at an angle to the mainmast.

Leaving Providence, Bill took the *Commencement* with only a small crew and sailed for Port Royal. Big Daniel, Adam, and most of the crew were back on Bill's island. Cat and her family had left weeks ago. The weather had been so bad that for the last few days, he had not even seen Jagua riding her dolphin alongside. Capturing Providence was not only a sound strategic move, it had also proven to be a windfall in supplying Bill and his men with the materials and armaments that they needed to fortify their secret island base. Bill loaded what livestock he wanted aboard ships and sailed them back to the island. He had his men disassemble all the equipment from the blacksmith and the cooper, the sailmaker and the rigger, the stonemason and the carpenter, and the cookhouses. Everything was crated and loaded aboard ships and sent to the island. The governor's house and the castle were both ransacked of everything of value—fine dishes and cutlery, furniture, rugs, drapes, paintings, books—everything was taken. Even clothing, shoes, and boots were taken.

Bill could have stolen more if time had allowed, but the privateers had held the island long enough. While they were well fortified and armed with ample provisions and in all probability could have held the fort against a Spanish attack, holding Providence was not Bill's plan. No, hit-and-run attacks is what Bill had preached to the Captains of the Coast.

"We don't fight conventional battles where the heavy guns of the Spanish galleons and their massive manpower of troops only serve the Spanish. We must pick our battles carefully. We hit where the Spanish least expect us. We seize a port, take everything, and leave."

Providence was only intended to be a staging point for the privateer fleets that were attacking up and down the Spanish Main. Once those fleets had been manned, equipped, and resupplied as needed, then there was no further need for Providence. It was abandoned.

Returning to his cabin, Bill spent the rest of the day mulling over in his mind what had happened.

"What have I accomplished during the last two years? It's almost unbelievable. I have captured all the Spanish nautical charts of the Caribe, I have in my hands all the detailed Spanish fortification plans, and I have secretly engaged Morgan to lead a fleet of privateers that are acting unknowingly on behalf of England. Lilly?" he said aloud, thinking. "She would be accepted back in England."

Unquestionably, she was the best choice, but Cat still plagued him. Thinking of returning to London with Lilly, Bill considered what Sir Harold had written him. He said that most of London has burnt to the ground. But the fires seemed to have cleansed the city of the worst of the plague. He had mentioned that even King Charles had been seen in the streets of the city fighting the fires. Between the plague and the fires, the city is devastated, Sir Harold wrote. But even before the fires had all been extinguished and the dead buried, the king and the merchants were busy drawing up plans to rebuild. The London of tomorrow, Sir Harold claimed, will be the greatest city in Europe.

Bill had a restless night.

The next morning, the sky had cleared somewhat, and Bill climbed the ratlines up to the masthead. The weather was warm and humid; the sky was dark, a brisk breeze filling the sails, pushing the ship through rough water. Bill liked climbing the mast and working the rigging high above the ship as he had done as a boy on his father's ships. It was where he thought best.

In the distance, Bill thought he saw something. At this height, he knew that he could spot the sails of another ship as far as forty miles away. A moment later, as Bill looked through his spyglass, he was sure. He saw the white tip of a sail dip under the purple-clouded horizon.

"On deck there!" he shouted to the men below. "On deck! Ship off the starboard beam, hull down." *Hull down* meant that Bill had only seen the sails that were visible above the horizon. The hull of the ship was below the horizon.

"Station watches aloft!" cried the boatswain.

Other men crawled into the rigging with Bill, trying to find the ship as it ducked in and out of the clouds and mist that covered the horizon. Several men now stationed in the rigging high above the deck also had spyglasses and peered across the endless blue waters. Suddenly, the distant ship came into focus clearly. Its course? Who was it, friend or foe?

"She be Spanish. A man-of-war she is!" shouted the first mate as he lowered his spyglass.

"Three-masted, third-rate ship of the line, by my eye!" shouted another.

"Cap'n," another man shouted, "there be more than one! I think I spy three more."

Bill saw the ships clearly now. They were warships, Spanish battleships. Three came into view, now a fourth, and finally the fifth ship flying the pennants of a Spanish flag admiral. It was Admiral Martinez de Palategui in the *Magdalena*. Martin was the only flag admiral that Bill knew of in these waters, and the *Magdalena* was a formidable warship on her own. The *Commencement* had no chance against the *Magdalena* if it came to an all-out fight.

"Their course?" Bill shouted back, now on the quarterdeck.

"They're closing in on us, Cap'n!" the man shouted. "They are coming across at us from different angles to our course."

Due to the unusual nature of the trade winds and the currents produced by the days of storms, the Spanish squadron of ships was not able to set a direct path of attack at the English vessel. The course of the hostile ships was upwind at parallel angles, aiming to where the wind or the current or both might take the ship at some future point. It was the old geometry lesson that Bill had learned under his father's tutorage. The Spanish fleet had probably picked them up as they left Providence and followed. But the storm hit, and they may have lost sight of the *Commencement*. But the same winds and currents that confounded Bill's ship also pushed the Spanish fleet in the same direction.

Martin was coming in behind the storm. He had probably spent days ducking back and forth below the horizon, always just out of sight, waiting for the weather to clear. Bill estimated that the Spanish warships, being heavier and therefore able to lay on full sail, would be much faster than the *Commencement* could bring to bear even if she was able to use all her sails, topgallants, and mizzen aloft. But the wind was too high for the shallow draft of the *Commencement*. She would heed over or lose a mast if all the sails were hoisted.

The closing distance rapidly diminished as Bill's vessel beat her way against the wind through the choppy water. It was still midmorning, and while Bill knew that they could not outrun the Spanish admiral's ships, he hoped that with a quarter moon that would not rise until eleven that evening, it just might be possible to escape in the night—if they could last that long.

"It's the Spanish admiral and his fleet," Bill said to Mr. Cribb, standing next to him on the quarterdeck. "Turn due south with the wind and lower two longboats."

When the longboats were lowered alongside, Bill shouted, "Set tar fires inside the boats and set them adrift! Smoke and oakum! It'll disguise our course with smoke. If we can make it until nightfall, there is still a chance that we can slip away in the darkness."

For hours the ship managed to stay just out of reach from the Spanish fleet by setting fires in the longboats and turning unexpectedly behind the smoke. But with each maneuver, they lost speed. And with the admiral's fleet advancing on all sides, it soon became apparent that a straight-out run was their only chance. But where were they going? Bill had been unable to fix a position for days. Which way should he run? *Will I be a lucky captain on this day?*

Hoping to run between Antigo or one of the other Windward Islands finding shallow waters, Bill ordered, "Due south!"

As the sun started to slip from the sky, Bill climbed back up the ratlines into the rigging for a better look. The Spanish always used the same battle plan. They never fired until they were at almost point-blank range. Then they would turn and fire a broadside with every cannon they had. The guns on the open gun deck would aim for the rigging. The cannons belowdecks, not able to elevate high enough to aim for the rigging, would fire at the waterline. Bill hoped that he could stay ahead of them, presenting only his stern. But a well-placed shot to the stern would cripple the rudder.

The first broadside from the Spanish admiral's guns lit the sky. Bill realized that one Spanish galleon was within a thousand yards. Bill saw the flash of orange and red light followed by the distant hollow groan of cannon blasts that he knew only too well. Twenty fourteen-pound cannons fired chain shots from the deck guns that cut through the *Commencement's* heavy masts, spars, and timbers. Heavy cannonballs also chopped apart the quarterdeck and blew wide holes across the stern. The rudder parted and fell into the water behind the ship. Bell-shaped balls connected by chain-wrapped projectiles cut through the rigging where Bill perched high above the deck. A hot piece of metal glanced off the mainmast and hit the side of his head. Pieces of hot metal and burning wood slivers dug into his chest, arms, and legs.

Bill fell one hundred feet into the sea below; his arms and legs were useless. Tangled in the broken spars, cordage, and sails, Bill plunged deep under the water in a dreamlike state. Only vaguely aware of what was happening to him, he watched as men died and his beloved *Commencement* sank. He was unable to react as he sank deeper and deeper under the water. Finally, after what seemed like an eternity, he slipped into unconsciousness.

Hoping to run between Antigo or one of the other Windward Islands finding shallow waters, Bill ordered, "Due south!"

As the sun started to slip from the sky, Bill climbed back up the ratlines into the rigging for a better look. The Spanish always used the same battle plan. They never fired until they were at almost point-blank range. Then they would turn and fire a broadside with every cannon they had. The guns on the open gun deck would aim for the rigging. The cannons belowdecks, not able to elevate high enough to aim for the rigging, would fire at the waterline. Bill hoped that he could stay ahead of them, presenting only his stern. But a well-placed shot to the stern would cripple the rudder.

The first broadside from the Spanish admiral's guns lit the sky. Bill realized that one Spanish galleon was within a thousand yards. Bill saw the flash of orange and red light followed by the distant hollow groan of cannon blasts that he knew only too well. Twenty fourteen-pound cannons fired chain shots from the deck guns that cut through the *Commencement's* heavy masts, spars, and timbers. Heavy cannonballs also chopped apart the quarterdeck and blew wide holes across the stern. The rudder parted and fell into the water behind the ship. Bell-shaped balls connected by chain-wrapped projectiles cut through the rigging where Bill perched high above the deck. A hot piece of metal glanced off the mainmast and hit the side of his head. Pieces of hot metal and burning wood slivers dug into his chest, arms, and legs.

Bill fell one hundred feet into the sea below; his arms and legs were useless. Tangled in the broken spars, cordage, and sails, Bill plunged deep under the water in a dreamlike state. Only vaguely aware of what was happening to him, he watched as men died and his beloved *Commencement* sank. He was unable to react as he sank deeper and deeper under the water. Finally, after what seemed like an eternity, he slipped into unconsciousness.

Postscript

She was off some point of land. The girl didn't know the name of the island or where she was exactly, but she carried the man onshore. The pounding waves broke in gushing white plumes of spray that filled the air with a translucent haze of mist. The glistening crystal-white sand sparkled under the moonlight like diamonds. Dark green palm fronds tumbled overhead in the wind, casting moving black shadows across the sand as she pulled the limp body of the man across the beach. She was a small woman with long oily black hair that hung to her hips. Her webbed toes clung to the unfamiliar feel of wet sand, and the thin membrane of pink webbed skin that spanned between her fingers just below the second knuckle held the man firmly as she crawled out of the water.

Was the man she had carried ashore still alive? She looked around the beach carefully. Sensing no one was there, the slim, muscular girl moved the man farther onto the beach. As she pulled his body behind her onto land the color of her skin seemed to be gradually changing with every step across the moonlit beach. The soft, gentle lines of her shoulder and back muscles changed first. Then her bare legs that were dusted with white sand gradually changed from a cool blue to a warm brown.

Her fingertips pressed to the man's neck felt the faint thread of life still running through his pale blue veins as she hovered over him. She put her ear to his bare chest. There was a dim heartbeat. Kneeling, she kissed the man with a warm breath that came from her soul.

With a deep gasp, the man she touched responded.

"Jagua," he whispered as his eyes opened briefly.

Taking a deep breath, he said again, "Jagua."